THE ANGEL'S SHARE

SATYAJIT SARNA graduated from the National Law School, Bangalore, in 2008. He lives in New Delhi. His poems were published in *First Proof: The Penguin Book of New Writing from India – 2*. He blogs at www.satyajitsarna.com.

the angel's share

SATYAJIT SARNA

HarperCollins *Publishers* India

First published in India by
HarperCollins *Publishers* in 2012
4th Floor, Tower A, Building No 10, DLF Cyber City,
DLF Phase II, Gurugram, Haryana – 122002
www.harpercollins.co.in

2 4 6 8 10 9 7 5 3

P-ISBN: 978-93-5029-333-1
E-ISBN: 978-93-5029-511-3

Typeset in 10.5/14 Sabon Roman at
SŪRYA

Printed and bound at
MicroPrints India, New Delhi

To my parents, who gave me dreams and the opportunities to chase them.

I asked if these two psychopaths could not be cured.

'Cured?' Goss said. 'Would you cure a singer of his voice?'

– *The Left Hand of Darkness*,
Ursula Le Guin, 1969

contents

imitation of life

R.E.M./Reveal/2001

After Sasha had died, the task of packing up his belongings was left to me. There wasn't much. I put his books and papers in his big black trunk, and his clothes and sheets in two suitcases, and handed them over to his parents. I kept one red shirt aside for Malaika, as I had promised, and swept the room out. Only one thing then remained – a pair of shin-guards Sasha had left leaning against the railing to dry. Hard yellow plastic with the brand paint peeling off, the foam on the inside discoloured with his sweat; a dead man's shin-guards. Those I kept for myself as an inadvertant bequest.

Sometimes, even now, I pull them out and look at them. Plastic is a sturdy thing. It does not rot or change. This is the truth we glean from archaeology – that our pots and pans and bangles and shin-guards will outlive us all.

More than anything, this is the story of Sasha Kapur and his short and brave life. If there were a way to tell this story fairly, I'd barely show up. I'd skim around the edges like a fruit fly, landing briefly on the scene and then buzzing away. And even if I was witness only to a little of his story, a handful of years, I feel bound to give testimony, because at times, I was the sole witness. If anyone else decides that they too should speak, let them come forward and step in the box.

One night, long ago, Sasha and I were lying on the smokers' slab of the Cauvery Hostel terrace. He was wearing only his football shorts, despite the fact that it was getting chilly, which puts us in approximately the autumn of 2002. Our campus, on the outskirts of Bangalore, was surrounded by miles of eucalyptus forest. From where we lay, it looked like a never-ending velvet carpet, over which some careless god had spilt patches of light.

'Zoju, I saw something in a movie yesterday.'

'What?'

'It was this movie with Goldie Hawn in it. She said something really interesting. Do you know why people get married?'

I was feeling unhelpful. 'Tax reasons. Lifetime free pass for random sex. Kids. Whatever else.'

'Yeah, but you can get all that in other ways. That's why people have sex or get into relationships or have kids. That's not why they get *married*. And even if those reasons are why they *got* married, that's not why they *stay* married.'

Sasha used to do this sort of fine semantic hair-splitting all the time.

'Fine. This is obviously a trick question. *You* tell me why people who don't even like each other stay married.'

'So, in this movie, Goldie Hawn's character says that it's because everyone needs a witness. Somebody who watches them live their life through.'

'That's just a little creepy. So you get married to some bitch you like, then you stop liking her and then she watches you for the rest of your life?'

'See, that's the point. The act of witnessing each other is the actual point of spending your whole life together. That's the magical part of the sacrament of marriage, tying two witnesses together.'

'Sounds delightful,' I said and rolled onto my back, but he wasn't listening. He had already started doing push-ups. Around that time, he was aiming to hit forty consecutively, which someone had told him was the Swedish army's minimum entry requirement. Why the Swedish army, an army that hadn't seen action in 200 years? Only Sasha knew.

Over the years, I've thought about what he said that night and I guess something stuck. Millions of us pass our lives under the stars, and most of us do the exact same things from day to day and live long gray neutral lives. So we get hitched to people so that somebody is contractually obligated to make us feel special, to witness the passage of the years, and to testify somehow. For those years, through no design of mine, I was privileged to be witness to Sasha's life.

We live our lives, muddling along, meat to the grinder, grain to the mill. But Sasha, he made his own road, burning for justice, lashing out at hypocrisy and lies and easy platitudes. Oh, don't get me wrong. More often than not, he was an asshole, an impetuous child, intemperate, churlish, sometimes intentionally hurtful and careless with people and things. But when he cared, more than anyone I've ever known, he wanted the world to be just. Even his childishness was an outpost of his reason. Why should anyone else care that he did not care what he wore, that he walked everywhere barefoot for weeks on end, that he spoke warmly with strangers and yet was incapable of small talk with anyone who mattered? We simply acknowledged that he was cheerfully insane and loved him for it, a uniquely jagged piece of the puzzle that was our lives.

Institutions can dream too, just like human beings, and gorillas and dolphins. In a sense, we were all part of one institutional dream in those years. We were all at the National Law School for our various reasons, some of us wanted to be lawyers, some of us had lawyer dads or moms, and the rest of us were there because you sat for every exam and took what you could get. I was there because the idea of being a lawyer seemed brighter than no idea at all.

I guess we all suffer from a fear that our experience is not unique; that everyone has the same things happen to them, that everyone feels unique, that the world turns and yet there is nothing new under the sun, that we pass the same stories back and forth. We fear this, yes, but we do not, we cannot believe it. Still, the more I talk to people from the IITs and other elite institutes, or people who went to India's great undergraduate liberal arts colleges, the more I see how different we were at Law School. I may be wrong, of course, but it seems to me that, back then, we were permissive in strange ways, restrained in others, rational to an irrational extent, more driven and pressure-cooked than anywhere else, less removed from the world and yet more removed from its gaze. We were promised the keys to the kingdom, but were never even told what the kingdom was.

To understand why, I suppose you have to look at the epistemology of the institution. Take one part Anglo-American liberal arts college, with its homoerotic Graeco-Roman heritage and interminable quest for the Truth. Add one part German technical institute, with its Teutonic backbone and commitment to producing professionals. Toss in two tablespoons of post-Nehruvian idealism and a pinch of postmodernism as seasoning, bake for fifteen years and garnish with the southern sunshine. Serve hot with cold lager.

Even after the lunar sadness of the end game, I cannot think of Law School with anything but warmth. It was still a young institution, vibrating with the different strokes it accommodated, when Sasha and I were there. Poverty and development activists, who were arrested for protesting big dams, coal mines, nuclear plants. Gay rights activists, trying to get the courts to read down Section 377 of the Indian Penal Code and allow them to joyfully bugger each other without being arrested for it. Constitutional and governmental theoreticians, feverishly rejigging concepts so big it was hard to see how they related to anything on the temporal plane. Feminists like Rohini, with her voluptuous body and melancholy eyes, so beautiful that she would make women angry and boys guilty. Corporate and commercial nuts so determined to serve money that they made it look noble. Even with all this in the air, it was a dreamy world, a paradise of pot, beer and sunshine, a culture of dissent and idiosyncratic actions, of practical jokes. You need jokers, madcaps, wild cards to disrupt the seriousness of all the discourse.

Here, you could start over. Read Althusser, become a poststructuralist for the weekend. Track down two photo exhibitions, become an art critic. Don't like who you are this week? Make yourself over, no one's going to hold it against you.

Into this world I entered, seventeen, fresh from school, ready to be something new, grasping at the opportunity to invent myself.

Now, let me recreate this fallen world, let me re-enchant myself and sweep aside the veil of the intervening years. It tears easily, because it is thin and porous.

Again, I remember the first time I walked into campus and down the flagstone path through the eucalyptus trees, the sunshine percolating through the trees, casting shadows of spear-shaped leaves on everything. The path led to a squat red building with white window ledges. I can smell again the chalky whitewash and sense the coolness of the dark corridor. It was then that I saw the inviting vision, the outstretched hand. At the heart of the white corridors, with a large open platform on one end, was a long lawn glowing in the sun like a green jewel. I felt my unease melt away like I had been waiting in the wings, and my cue had finally come.

The medical check-up took place at a small clinic in town. After the doctor had hit me on the back a few times, used the hammer on my knee and made me open my mouth wide, I found myself in a toilet with a pair of little medical cylinders and a wooden ice cream spoon, producing urine and stool samples. When I closed the door after me, carrying my cargo a little self-consciously, I bumped into a short girl with shoulder-length hair and glasses, coming out of the adjacent toilet stall.

'Sorry.'

'It's okay. Are you from NLS?'

'Yes. Umm, my name is Malaika.'

'I'm Zorawar. I'd normally shake your hand, but ...'

She grabbed my hand with a sudden jerky movement and leaned forward a little, her eyes wide.

'I can't believe they made us shit in a box!'

Within a few minutes, I had already met four more people who were going to sit in class with me for the next five years. In retrospect, it seems to me that it – all of us lined up by roll number, holding our little boxes of shit – should have served as a portent.

As I approached my room in the evening, I noticed that the door was open and Carnatic music was playing. I was greeted by the sight of a bespectacled young man in a stiff white shirt and a dhoti sweeping out the room. He looked up and blinked.

'Umm ... Hello?'

'Hi. I'm Seshadri. Seshadri Ramachandran.'

'Zorawar Chauhan. I suppose we're roommates.'

'Yes. I'm sure we are. Listen, I'm sorry about the lock. I broke it because I didn't know when you were coming and, as you know, time and tide wait for no man. Anyway, I have a few extra locks. Please take one.'

Enter Mr Seshadri Ramachandran, my roommate. The sort of guy who owns extra locks. Good Tamil boy. Gets stiff when he smells sambar.

Our room was shaped like a T, with three equal-sized divisions. Each of the cubicles had a window with bars and a mesh screen, and a small brown wooden cupboard built into the wall, below which there were two bare cement racks. A third of the room was taken up by a brown metal cot, with two T-shaped rods attached at the head and foot to hold up a mosquito net. A metal desk of the same despondent brown sat under the window. I would have called it spartan, if only it were better furnished.

I retired to my cubicle, placed my mattress on the bed and my blanket on the mattress. Then I unpacked my suitcases and stowed them under the bed. I sat on my bed and surveyed my cubicle. The walls were bare, the cupboard was half-full, the cement rack held two pairs of shoes and a pair of bathroom slippers. There was a picture of the family on the desk and there were biscuits in the drawer. I switched off the light.

Suddenly, an overpowering loneliness swept over me. I slipped my legs inside the blanket and looked up at the brown fan, which was circling slowly at its one speed. There was some laughter coming through the window, but it had nothing to do with me. If only I could walk out of the door and into my house in Delhi, into my own room, where my old life waited. I'd put it on like a comfortable old pair of jeans and be happy.

The lights in the next cubicle went off as well.

'Umm … Goodnight, Zorawar?'

'Goodnight, Seshadri.'

Silence.

'Umm … Zorawar, when do you like to wake up in the morning?'

'I generally get up by seven-thirty, quarter-to-eight. Why?'

'Okay. I'll wake you up then? I get up at six o'clock to do my prayers.'

'Alright then. Goodnight.'

'Goodnight, Zorawar.'

Well, it wasn't my mother, but at least someone here was praying. Some things were the same as home. I would manage, I thought, and went to sleep for a few hours.

At two in the morning, the relentless knocking on the door woke us up. Seshadri and I opened the door together, blinking in the corridor light. Standing outside, grinning brightly, was a short *kid* who looked about fourteen, with close-cropped hair and a bright orange shirt. He had behind him a trunk with neat white stencilling on it and a big blue duffel bag.

'Hi!' he said, a little too loudly. 'I'm Sasha Kapur. Can I come in?'

Without waiting for a response, he strode in, whistling and dragging his things behind him. He turned on the light, looked around approvingly, moved the bed from one side of the room to the other. He then jumped up and touched the fan. As I watched – for Seshadri had wordlessly gone back to sleep – he unpacked his clothes and stuff in minutes and changed without the slightest embarrassment into a pair of bright white pyjamas. Sasha then held his right hand up to his nose and seemed to smell it while rubbing his forefinger over his thumbnail in a circular motion.

'What's your name?'

'Zorawar.'

'Grand name. Sorry for the trouble, but my taxi got lost. I barely managed to convince the guards to let me in.'

'Why do you do that?' I pointed at his thumb and forefinger.

'This? I'm doing this so I can have hard shiny thumbnails. See?'

I looked at the thumbnail presented to me. It shone like mother of pearl.

'Right,' I said and, having run out of conversation, 'I'm going back to sleep. Goodnight.'

'Goodnight, don't let the bedbugs bite.'

Who says that? I wondered, and then quit trying to figure out my new roommate and went back to sleep.

In the morning, I bathed and dressed early and headed off to the mess for breakfast. The mess counter had on it a stack of plates and two huge steel pots. In the first was a white grainy mass with little leaves and nuts in it. The second one was a sun yellow mass dotted with raisins and covered with an inch of oil. Clearly a halwa of some sort. I took a ladleful from each bowl and sat down at the first-years' table.

'Hey,' the rotund bespectacled guy across the table said, pointing a fat finger at the plate. 'Do you know what they call that?'

'Upma? Halwa?'

'No,' he said with relish, 'that's what you call it. What do NLS students call it?'

'I have no idea.'

'I heard some guy on that table call it white shit/yellow shit, with the slash pronounced.'

'Oh,' I reconsidered the palette of my plate. Then, nothing ventured, nothing gained, I attacked it with the spoon. 'What's your name?'

'Amlan,' he said, mournfully. I noticed that the grease on his glasses carried his fingerprints. 'My deepest fear is that we're looking at five years of white shit/yellow shit.'

After breakfast, I returned to the room to pick up my notebook. I had a full forty minutes before class began.

Seshadri was out of the room. Sasha was dressing. I watched him go about his business, humming to himself. I then thought I could use the opportunity to take a quick nap instead.

'Sasha, I'm just going to sleep for a little bit. Wake me up before you leave for class?'

'Sure,' he said and sounded comfortingly sympathetic. 'I must have disturbed your sleep last night. I'm sorry.'

'Hardly. Don't mention it.' What a sweet guy, I thought, what a gem, and closed my eyes.

When I awoke an hour later, in a sweaty panic, the room was empty. I pulled my pants on frantically and ran to the door. I pulled on it, and it did not budge. It was obviously locked from the outside. I banged on it, and screamed to my heart's content, and only the uncaring walls of the hostel heard me.

Resigned to my fate, I returned to bed, cursing Sasha. I wondered what I was missing behind that brown door. Wasn't the first lecture supposed to be the most important? Would I ever be able to figure anything out? What did my classmates look like? What were classrooms like? Teachers?

When Seshadri finally unlocked me after class, I nearly mauled him out of curiosity. What had we learnt in the four hours I was locked in?

'Nothing, Zorawar. Nothing new. Same old things. Socratic Method. Buddhist parable of the elephant and the blind men. Discourses and narratives. Nothing special. Disappointing, really.'

'Nothing new at all?'

'Nothing new for a smart guy like you.'

Naturally, I did not ask for any clarifications from Seshadri – too much of my reputation lay at stake. I asked

Amlan later what all of those things were. Amlan explained them as follows:

A. Socratic Method: 'When in doubt, ask questions. When not in doubt, ask anyway.'
B. Buddhist parable: 'Bunch of blind men feel up an elephant. Can't figure out what it is. Because they're blind. Someone tells them later. They're damn surprised.'
C. Discourses and narratives: 'Things people say are discourses. Alternately, they are narratives.'

It did not appear to me that I had missed much on my first day of Law School.

In my room, not many days later, Rathore expounded a Corollary to the Socratic Method. Picture a thin and clean-limbed young man in a pair of boxers with a rudraksh mala around his neck, the beads tangling with his curly chest hair. His long, aristocratic nose flared and his eyes were wide and tinged with red. Over his shoulder was a thin towel that smelt like correction fluid. In his hand was a box of powdered milk that my mother had packed for me, which Rathore was in the process of consuming with a spoon. Between spoonfuls, he spoke sonorously.

'Young first year, what is it they put in this to make it taste so good? Why is it so much better than cow-tit milk?'

'I don't know.'

Rathore's eyes widened in shock. 'You don't know? That's terrible. You have owned this box for nearly a week, and you have no idea?'

'No. Not really.'

'Do you have any idea at all?'

'No.'

'Then why do you say "not really", as if you have some idea.' A disturbing thought struck him. 'Are you trying to fuck with me, first year?'

'No. No. Absolutely not.'

'Good, what a relief. Which means that you speak inexactly out of habit and don't read the sides of boxes. Never mind.' He laid a hand absently on my shoulder. 'You will learn. Did they tell you about the Socratic Method?'

'Yes.'

'What do you think it means?'

I phrased my answer carefully. 'It means that you have to ask questions to understand things.'

Rathore was horrified. 'My god, what a terribly simplistic way of teaching you anything at all. You first years are, intellectually speaking, the scum that accumulates at the bottom of cess-pits. Does your mother think you are very intelligent?'

'Yes.'

'Good. That's one person. Now, first year, before I go to my room and pass out, I'm going to lay some knowledge on you. The Socratic understanding of life is underpinned by one particular thesis. Which is ...' He threw his hands up in the air and boomed, 'The Unexamined Life is Not Worth Living.'

I looked at him and tried to take the next step. 'Which means that we should all ask questions and enquire into everything, to better know the life we live.'

Rathore tilted his head and looked at me coldly. 'Why are you yapping like a little puppy, first year? If you don't know anything, you should keep your mouth shut and not subtract from the sum of human knowledge.'

He closed his eyes, wrapped the towel around his mouth and nose and breathed in, his thin pale chest expanding like a balloon.

'Now, you idiot, why would you want to examine *everything*? There are truly terrible things on this planet. Coal mines, homosexuals, jholawallahs, Kannadigas, hard work, procedural law. Why on earth would you want to examine these? That is the question that you should ask yourself.' Triumphantly, Rathore tossed the empty box of milk powder onto my bed. 'Instead, you must seek to know good things. Music, women, drugs, alcohol, all of which are good things. It is your duty to come to know these things better. That is the meaning of the examined life. Therefore, your highest dictum should be The Only Life Worth Living is the Good Life.'

I thought about it and saw no flaws in his reasoning. 'You're right.'

'Huh?' Rathore was lost in thoughts of his own, which seemed to find an answer in the ceiling. 'What? First years, I don't even know why I waste my time on you.'

Rathore wandered out with his face in his towel. Socrates had started making a great deal of sense to me. I looked forward to better grasping his method. After all, college really was supposed to be about intellectual stimulation.

at the chime of a city clock

Nick Drake/Bryter Layter/1970

More than five years after the night that Sasha walked into my life, I have now walked through a fresh door. They said they'd put me on a deal soon enough, but I haven't had any work to do yet. I've been sitting here in my new suit, silk tie around my neck, jacket on my chair. There's a phone at my desk with shortcut buttons for all the members of the capital markets team, and a terminal to the network. A nameplate hangs off my cubicle wall. Zorawar Chauhan, it says in neat sans serif, Associate. This is my new home.

The New Delhi offices of Lawrence & Kamraj Associates is a pastry of pistachio greens and sombre ochres. If you had to label it, I suppose you could call it moderne – the same materials they use worldwide to signify business; the wooden floors, the brushed paint walls, the frosted glass panels in the conference rooms, the nameless abstract art and a tip-of-the-hat to a nebulous Indian tradition.

All the windows on this floor are on one side, where the partners' cabins are, so you can't really tell the time of day. The office sounds like money – money being made and money being spent. Keyboards clack in symphony, phones ring constantly, juniors run to the copy machine, to partners' cabins, to conference rooms. The heels of shoes click smartly on floor tiles. Opinions are being issued, emails are being sent, documents are being produced and reviewed. This ship sails on a sea of paper, leaving behind a trail of signatures, assents and comments.

The capital markets partner at LKA Delhi is Abhilash Devrath. He's a short, stout man, hard and pale like he got a litre less blood than the rest of God's children. The rumour is that nobody has ever seen him eat; that he survives on alcohol, cigarettes and energy bars. Abhilash isn't forty yet, but his face is lined with care and there are perpetual dark circles under his eyes. He wears ties so red they spell trouble. On his desk is an economy size bottle of hand sanitizer that he pumps at compulsively. When you pass his cabin, he's usually on the phone and cleansing his hands. When he is correcting drafts, he leans forward till his face is inches from the page, and flips his tie over his shoulder so it doesn't drag on the table. He uses a pencil from his pencil stand – and all of his pencils are the same colour, the same make and, somehow, of the same length.

The one time I saw him leave his room, he strode over to a cubicle in the middle of the floor and dropped a stack of papers on some associate's desk. His voice was loud and hard like a slap.

'You've had a whole week to work on this. After one week on a draft, I expect a Rolls Royce. As usual, you've given me a fucking scooter.'

I made up my mind right then to make sure I never gave Abhilash a scooter.

I'm so lucky to be here, to have landed this job, the one we dreamt of for all those years. Piles of money, the biggest deals in the country, headlines in *The Economic Times*, business lounges, credit cards with concierge services. It's all mine now. It ought to have been beyond my reach, with my abysmal grades and my patchy CV. But the Sensex was cracking 22,000, and every industry but cement was showing positive indicators. At recruitment time, they came to the main gate, backed their truck up and loaded in first-year associates. I wriggled in and, now, here I am, getting comfortable.

I plan to start over. I promise myself that this will be different. I'm going to work harder. I'm not going to compromise on quality. I'll put in the extra mile, the hardest lap and make sure I get it right. If everyone else leaves at eight, I'll put in an hour more and leave at nine.

This is the new game and there's no ceiling. If I warm up, train hard, stay patient, I can make partner in six years, date models, give interviews to the pink papers. I can have the keys to the world markets, which never sleep, which roil and froth across the globe. I can have it all.

one stage before

Al Stewart/Year of the Cat/1979

When I came to college, I was a year younger than most of our batch and a year at eighteen is endlessly long. Everyone seemed to have the edge over me in every way, was made of some more durable thing.

It wasn't just Sasha's courage and freedom from doubt that I desired. It was the perfection of his uniqueness. Even his name was one of a kind – a freak chance of birthplace and heritage. Sasha's dad was an officer of the Indian Navy and, when Sasha was born, he was posted in Vladivostok, then in the Soviet Union. The port of Vladivostok on the North Sea, a place so cold that the concept of a variable climate is the difference in temperature between ice and icy water. Sasha was named after an old orderly on the local staff, a man whose eyes were grey and blue like the bits of the sea that were not frozen over and whose beard was white like the parts that were.

Names were always a game with Sasha. For example, he had a dog named Brutus, whom he called Mukeshwaran.

That's Mukeshwaran, with an extended ook and a soft r – Mookeyshwaran.

'Why Mukeshwaran, da?' I asked one day. Sasha was lighting a stick of incense to clear our room of smoke.

'It's a nice native name. Brutus is so … bourgeois. Rocky, Jackie, Blacky, Brutus.'

'Dude, you can't compare Rocky, Blacky type names with Brutus! Brutus is a noble name.'

'So is Mukeshwaran.' He crooned it to himself lovingly, closing his eyes and pouting. 'Moookeyshwarrran. Zojeshwarran.'

'Huh? How am I Zojeshwaran?'

'Simple. No one should call you Zorawar. It has too much gravitas. Maybe later, when you're older. You'll grow into it. Your short name is Zoju.'

'Okay, fine. But how do you get from that to Zojeshwaran?'

'You just append a suffix to the name. Eshwaran for male. Eshwari for female. If the name ends with a vowel, you get rid of it, and then it ends with a consonant.'

'So, Tomeshwaran, Dickeshwaran, Harreshwaran?'

'Yeah. And then, if you want to shorten it, just go back to the esh. Like, Zojesh.'

'Wow. There's five minutes of my life I'll never get back,' I said, getting out of bed and searching for pants.

But the names stuck. People began using them unconsciously. First as mockery, then irony and, eventually, it became culture.

It wasn't just Sasha, though, there was something special about everyone here.

Take Seshadri, who was effortlessly smarter than I was. I'd been used to being the brightest spark around, ever since

I had come into the education system, easily pulling down high test scores, topping the school in science, having teachers tell me I was such a bright lad. It was such a bitter comedown to be faced with Seshadri's intellect. When I saw him breezing through bits of Lyotard about the postmodern condition, and comfortably negotiating subtle jurisprudential distinctions, I knew that I had come across a brain I could not match. If Seshadri had the social graces of a concrete mixer, or the athleticism of a concrete mixer, or the physical beauty of a concrete mixer, it didn't matter. The man who can synthesize an understanding of the world *that* perfect can place himself wherever he pleases within it. Seshadri was destined for the absolute upper echelons of the world. Almost every year, NLS graduated one Rhodes scholar, and we all knew where Seshadri would be toddling off to at the end of five years.

I wanted to be cool like Raghav, to be at ease anywhere and to know how to talk to everyone. The gift of confidence, the ability to transform any scene you enter into your star turn, so everyone else is reduced to supporting cast. In the first year, Raghav had already seen and done so much. He was a killer football player, had a girlfriend off-campus, had a car of his own in Bombay, and came fully acquainted with sex, drugs and rock and roll. To me, it seemed like he had the world in the palm of his hand. I wanted his feet, his ability to extract a football from a crowd, to pervert a defensive situation. I wanted the ease with which he slipped a shirt over his athletic body. I wanted the ability to look good wearing only boxers. Most of all, I wanted his situation, where he did not need to want.

That's not all I wanted. Those who aren't given everything on a platter have to fight for it, work for it, run for it.

Nobody did that better than Kelkar. He believed that if he worked hard enough, he could have everything. It sounds admirable until you know how psychotic the depth of that belief was – how much anger he had bottled up in him, channelled like that. It had taken two broken marriages to create him, a home so fucked up that he grew bent inward like a plant contained in a box, shaped like his restrictions.

Kelkar worked like a dog to get the grades he did. In those five years, no one did more background reading than Kelkar, his table lamp on late into the night. In the morning, he'd look dark and ragged but, the next night, he'd be up again. With that same intensity, he ran and trained to make the college team, running every day and practising goal kicks into the evening. Of course, if you are that hungry, that fuelled by rage, you're never fully confident of your ability, never fully secure. And so, God forbid you got around Kelkar, you'd be scythed down so hard that he'd be standing up before you had stopped falling. Sasha once told him as much: 'Kelkar, I'm going to call you Succedeshwaran.' He crooned it out lovingly, as he took his shin-guards out of his stockings.

'Why?' Kelkar squinted through his glasses.

'Because it doesn't matter when you start anything, you'll succeed at it sooner or later, even if you're ugly and graceless.'

'Fuck you, da. I only seem graceless because I'm taller than you and this is a short man's game.'

But there was more to him than determination and grit; the more time you spent with him, the more he felt like a bear trap, jaws held apart by a fragile spring or bending stick. He told me once about how that trap had snapped when he was a child. A stray pup had wandered into his yard and taken a shit. The grey and yellow goop that animals shit when they're eating garbage lay stinking in the sun and incensed him. Maybe there was more to it than a puddle of shit, maybe his stepdad had been around more than usual, maybe someone had been shouting, but Kelkar followed that puppy down the street, chased it into an alley where some construction was always happening and wedged it into a corner with a wooden board. Then he picked up half-bricks and chunks of rock and stoned the dog till its skull cracked open and it stopped moving. He says he did a couple of years of counselling after that, but I can't say for sure that it did him much good. So no, maybe I don't want Kelkar's ability to focus, not at that price.

I even wished I had Amlan's pride. Amlan was lazy, like me, and not gifted at a whole lot of things and cursed generously by fate with blubber and allergies. But he compensated with delusional self-regard. On the inside, perhaps he chewed himself thin like an old toothbrush. But on the outside, he had an armour coat of attitude – a layer of nihilism and confrontation that made him seem strong. Amlan was a guy so dark, so offensively depressing, that if he ever condescended to go to a therapist, he'd get charged double.

'Kelkar,' he said, unprompted, at Five Buck Shop, exhaling smoke, 'you know what your problem is?'

'I don't have any problems. I'm perfect. I'm a Big Man.'

'One of your many problems then. You may be an effective football player, but you will never be a good football player.'

Kelkar's temper was rising, but he wanted to reason it out. 'If I'm effective, then I'm fulfilling the goals of the game, no? That makes me a good player of the game. So proven.'

'No, you see, it is a spectator sport. And you have to look good when you play. Like Sasha; he plays well and he looks natural and graceful. You have a … spring in your step, but you don't have grace.' He ashes his cigarette.

'So, I not only have to play my position well, play my role in the team well and be a good sportsperson. I also have to look good to you? You who doesn't even play the sport, who doesn't even watch it on television.' Kelkar's face is turning red. 'Amlan, please tell me what the offside rule is? Please, just give me the gist of it.'

'Never mind. It's only a rule. This isn't about me – it's about you. There's no requirement to be an educated spectator. But you have to play gracefully, so that you please spectators. Else, why bother?' With that, he extinguished his cigarette triumphantly. 'See you later.'

He swung his leg over his Yamaha Rx 100 and, waving indulgently at an apoplectic Kelkar, zipped into the distance.

Of us all, Kiran was the closest to being an actually normal person, well adjusted, mentally whole. He was more everyman than any of the rest of us. Where Kelkar had rage issues, Amlan was manic-depressive, Raghav was cynical and world-weary and Sasha was just plain bonkers, the oddest thing you could say of Kiran was that he was a little bit pervy. His porn collection was a curator's delight, sorted alphabetically by text, image and video. Each file also bore a considered rating out of ten and the whole thing was added to and backed up regularly. But, even in that, he was not unusual except in his earnestness and, of all the world's sins, that of Onan is the easiest forgiven.

I envied Kiran his natural grace, his slim brown frame, light as a kite. The way his abdominal muscles rippled in his stomach like billiard balls. His was not the strength to act as a force in the world, to move heavy objects, or to absorb great impacts, but he was always master of every movement of his limbs, always able to dictate the graceful and deft turn, to control his own life well.

It showed on the field. Kiran had the viperous touch of an Inzaghi, to get some edge of himself to the ball in the box and to poke it home. The ball would roll in to the box, take a deflection and pass through the crowd at an odd height – at our level of play, these things would happen a lot. At the end of that odd travel, Kiran would have burst through to get to the point where the ball would ricochet off his shin into the post and then spin across the line cussedly.

I also envied Kiran his social ease, his ability to move beyond his friends at unwieldy, large occasions without leaving them behind. He found it so easy to seek out distant relatives in the city and become part of the family. I remember accompanying him to a party at an army mess, where we were stuck behind the bar by his uncle. We handed out strong gin and vodka cocktails masked crudely with guava juice – which undoubtedly caused some puzzled soul-searching among the guests the morning after – and laughed about it all the way back on his old green motorcycle. We reached the centre of the city and paused at a red light on the road running past the Sacred Heart Cathedral. I stood up to adjust my pants and he accelerated away when the light changed. Only 200 feet later did he realize that his 80cc bike was behaving suspiciously powerful. When he turned around, he saw me standing outside a house of worship, abandoned and yelling like a madman.

Because Kiran was my friend, he came back to get me. Something I should have remembered.

diamonds & rust

Joan Baez/Diamonds & Rust/1975

Maybe it's true for everyone, that there are those nights we think of as magic, when everything goes right and every uncertainty leads to an unforeseen and sublime outcome.

It was 10.30 p.m. on a winter night halfway through our first year. The auto had brought Sasha and me to Kanakpura Road, dark and wet, with trees hanging over it on both sides. We hadn't seen a car in five minutes and the signs that we were told to look out for – the school, the silk farm – hadn't appeared yet. The autowallah was raking it in, the meter had turned over twice. And then, out of nowhere, a little bit of paint on a rock, a hand-painted sign that said Eco Village. We dismounted and continued down the dirt track on foot, which brought us to a bridge above a whispering stream, beyond which hummed a small power station. I was slightly worried.

'This doesn't look like the sort of place you'd have a rock show.'

'Well, there's no point turning back now, is there?'

Which was fair. It was eleven at night and we were walking down this mud track in the middle of nowhere. The auto was long gone. The little A4 poster in Pecos had provided a date and a place, and not much more. We walked into a long stretch of field broken only by coconut trees, the grass was knee high and the lights of the power station had faded to a diffused glow. The track had disappeared. Then, when we were in the *precise* centre of nowhere, we heard the repetitive vibration of drums. Which is how we found the Rainseed Festival, an amber jewel in the Elysian night.

A small amphitheatre set in the middle of a bunch of cottages in the wilderness, where bamboo groves fell away to reveal a still pond. We had not come unprepared; a bottle of whisky came out of the bag Sasha was carrying. Seconds later, a hand descended on his back. We turned around expecting some form of authority and met only a familiar grin. It was Kelkar.

'Sasha! Zojeshwaran! How it is?'

Rohini had brought Kelkar, Seshadri and quiet little Jennifer; perhaps a mothering urge for her; for the two boys at least, it was part hero worship and part lust. The lake was a mirror to the sky, every tree, every reed and frond etched into its silvery surface. We sat there, listening to the bands play, booming over the trees. After two insipid blues bands and one painful death metal band, Thermal and a Quarter took the stage. In the warm yellow light, Thermal's funk-infused rock, the bass humming like a giant rubberband in the sky, was tantric, songs in the key of sex.

At three o'clock, the lights went out when the generator ran out of gas and the warm yellow light was replaced by white moonlight. The music cut out abruptly. At any rate, there were scarcely ten people left in the audience.

The guitarist coughed. 'Well, that's the end of our electric set. Sing along, anyone?' He rummaged around for an acoustic. In the drunken moonlight, even retarded songs, cheesy songs sound good, like the patina of bullshit had been scraped clean off them. The sing along that night was rough, stop-start, un-rehearsed and utterly unforgettable.

Love is a long and slippery process. But sometimes you can identify the moment when someone becomes worth loving. For me, that moment was when Jennifer asked, in a small clear voice, maybe the first time I heard it, 'Do you know "Diamonds and Rust"?'

In that clearing, under the moon, she sang high and warm, like deep bells in the hills, 'Well I'll be damned/Here comes your ghost again'.

You can forgive some people their pride and self-centredness, because they actually are more interesting than other people. That's why we have great poets who can write about trivial shit and people read it. Why Joan Baez could write a bitchy overwrought song like 'Diamonds and Rust' and, yet, when sung by a voice like Jennifer's, it can consume the heart of a boy sitting on a patch of grass.

Sitting there, my head in Sasha's lap, looking up at her frame, I was consumed with envy and lust and a feeling of slipping. Her voice crept across the grass like thieves stealing from fields, taking possession of everything in its way. I held myself still, wanting the moment to drive on forever into the beautiful silver future. When she finished, she looked at me.

The next morning, when the sun came up over the palm trees, sleepy and grouchy, with our hair tousled and clothes rumpled, we walked back through the fields, past the watching farmers who were having their breakfast. On the turn to the main road, holding out our thumbs, we flagged down a truck and rode back to town on a bed of straw in the sunny rural morning.

I miss nights like that. I miss pushing through moshpits drunkenly, across to the barricades where you could headbang and bump into strangers. Every night, we trusted in a preserving god to hold us and guide us, when our reason and sense of self-preservation had failed us. And how that god would care for us, on the nights we took buses and rickshaws, or hitched rides to get to the middle of nowhere for festivals, islands of lit tents in hundreds of miles of darkness and villages, connected to the world by narrow threads of unpaved road. At the end of every long night, or at its beginning, I miss landing up at Pecos, the greatest little rock and roll bar in India.

When the bomb dropped, Kelkar and I were at Pecos, looking at the bottom of our second pitcher and calculating whether we could afford a third and still get back to college. The barman had just put on some Credence. Behind Kelkar's head, Jerry Garcia strummed a guitar in black paint. I had my feet up on a stool and my back against a brick wall covered with years of scratched names and messages. The management had gotten sick of repainting it, and so it marked out a history of Pecos regulars; lots of Law School students. An empty dish of ghee roast pork lay greasily beside a bowl of cold unpopped kernels of popcorn. Kelkar was waxing lyrical about all the places he wanted to go to: Prague, Caracas, Istanbul, all of which had the chief virtue of being home to ridiculously hot women. Kelkar dreamt of travel, and still dreams of it, constantly. It's like he's searching for the realities that black-and-white pictures are drawn from, the source material of *Life* photographs. He sees continents full of old men playing chess, lovers out in the afternoon sun, cafés where no one takes off their sunglasses or puts out their cigarette. Every window frames a beautiful sad woman, every alley guards a secret.

The call came from Seshadri, which itself was odd, given that Seshadri messaged rather than called, if he ever needed to. The gesture violated his natural parsimony. 'Where are you?' he asked.

'Pecos, machan.'

'Hmmm. When are you getting back?'

'Soon only. What's up?'

'Nothing. No hurry, but come to the Acad block when you get back.'

When we did get back, we saw Malaika sitting on the steps outside sobbing, her head between her knees. She motioned us to the Exam Department. The day we had been dreading was here. First trimester results were out.

When I fought my way to the sheet tacked up on the wall, the results tab for Sociology, Legal Methods and Economics were all up. So, B+ in Socio, disappointing. A in Legal Methods! Great! And Economics?

My eyes swam down the row of names and numbers. The grades on the side were swathes of Fs and Bs and not much above that. And there, against my name, an F. The letter manifested with such immanence that I felt this was the first time I had seen it.

It was my first F, of course. All forty Fs on the Economics gradesheet belonged to people who'd never failed a thing in their lives, there was no other sort at Law School. The blow hit us all like a wet papier-mâché fist. How do you tell your parents you've flunked an introductory course in Economics?

Kelkar had just passed everything by the skin of his teeth and was bitter about it. Seshadri had Outstandings in Economics and Legal Methods and a B+ in Sociology, and was furiously muttering under his breath. Everyone had taken a hit, but to *fail*?

I found Amlan smoking a cigarette at the gate. He seemed calm. 'I'm leaving college,' he said.

'Why?' I asked, snagging a cig out of his shirt pocket.

'I got ninety-two per cent in CBSE twelfth. If I can't even pass Socio I, then nothing can be done here. What's the point of staying?'

'I flunked Economics. Some people flunked all three.'

'But I don't measure myself by those standards. I topped my class for six years.'

'Well, Seshadri didn't and he's got two Os. Things are different here. We'll all just pass in the repeats.'

'What if we don't?' Amlan lit a fresh cigarette off the end of the last one.

'Carry-overs. You can take three from a year to the next one.'

Amlan laughed bitterly. 'If you're not good enough to pass the first two times you give a fucking exam, there's no chance you'll pass the third time.' Amlan exhaled, leaning his head on the ivy behind him. 'In fact, if you can't pass Economics I, Zojo, why would you believe that you can pass Economics II,' he laughed, 'or Corporate or Tax or any of the law subjects that are based on Economics?'

I was silent, considering the enormity of the task that lay before us. Were we good enough to be here at all? Did we luck out last year, and would we end up flunking out by next year?

It was getting dark. 'Come,' said Amlan. 'I'm out of fags and we need to go study for the repeats.'

We studied for and passed those repeats, and swore we'd never find ourselves in that position again. Next trimester, we studied for new repeats. It settled in, gradually, like a shawl around your shoulders. Once you've given one repeat, you'll give others, your grades will cement about a point and stick there. As the years pass, it gets harder to move that point in any direction. When we graduated, we all probably had the same grade point average as we had that first trimester.

charmless man

Blur/The Great Escape/1995

So you've been up till two in the morning, running the draft, working in comments from the bankers, the bankers' counsel and Abhilash. Then you mail it out, taking great pride in marking everyone in the working group list, so as to point out that you work all the time. Go home. Wake up at five so that you can make the first flight out to Bombay at 6.50 a.m. It's dark and the night is clammy with waiting sweat.

You hit Bombay at nine and roll out of Chhatrapati Shivaji to the cab waiting for you. At 9.30, you're at the company's offices. You unbutton your jacket and hand out your business card ve-e-ery carefully. Both hands, slight bow, index fingers below and thumbs above. When you receive a business card, you give that two-handed bow again. It's the Japanese way and everyone's so impressed with it that they've adopted it. Then you take the time to properly appreciate the card. 'Hmm,' you say, 'Assistant

Vice President – Finance,' obviously impressed at the mad dash up the ladder the presenter must have executed to have reached this exalted position at only thirty years of age. And then, at last, in roll the bankers, with their strolleys and Berries.

Frankly, I wouldn't know how to deal with all of these people if it wasn't for Dhruv, whom I'm accompanying on this trip. He's only three years my senior, but he's done dozens of deals, logged enough miles to circumnavigate the world three times at the equator and has his thumb perpetually on the scroll button of his Berry. He looks the part. Pinstripes, nice ties, thick framed spectacles, a little belly roll, the sort of chin that slopes gently away to his neck. The picture builds itself, doesn't it? You can almost smell the competitiveness that comes from being a schoolyard runt. It shouldn't surprise you that he has a Rottweiler. It should still astound you that he's taught it to salute him.

After the meetings, we check into the hotel, and Dhruv knows the lobby manager and the lobby manager knows him by first name. He introduces me. 'Rakesh, meet my colleague, Zorawar. Zorawar, this is the most important man in Bombay.'

The manager smiles unctuously and we are ushered up to our rooms. The linen is spotlessly white and everything smells like lemongrass. I look into the bathroom and there is a bathtub, which I plan to spend the night in. From my window, I can see all of Marine Drive stretching out like a neon dream.

Dhruv tells me to come down for a drink at the bar. At the bar, Dhruv knows the bartender. He keeps talking about the one time he came to the bar and got plastered on these '*wicked* drinks, man'. We order two.

'You missed a real party last year, Zoju. Lawrence's daughter got married.'

'Oh okay.'

'Yeah, you should have seen it. There were all these different bars and killer bartenders. There was this one bar with just whiskies. Forty single malts, and a cigar humidor.'

'Wow.'

'And you should have seen the guest list. All the bigwigs from the Supreme Court. Ratan Tata. Uday Kotak. Both Ambani brothers.'

'Both of them were there? I thought they couldn't be in a room together.'

'Oh, they weren't,' he grinned. 'One left, and then the other came.'

Two more drinks. Mine had that thick creamy froth that comes on a perfectly shaken drink.

'I want you to really bust your ass on this deal, Zoju. Abhilash wants to give you a proper run out. He thinks you can be a star for this team, you can really sell the deal. He thinks you have that spark.'

I resolve to run my legs off. Suddenly, it's like the weariness from the late night and the all-day meeting just melts away.

The bartender does tricks with the shaker and whacks the caps of beer bottles with a wooden paddle. And Dhruv points to the women glittering in the warm yellow lights. 'Don't you love the tits on that one, Zorawar? Hey, look, she looked at you. Give her a shot, bro.'

I decline and, as we leave, Dhruv tips the bartender five hundred bucks. For a second, I am shocked, because that would have taken care of an entire night of drinking for a bunch of us at Surya. I realize that the scale has changed, that you can tip five hundred bucks on a five grand tab.

After Dhruv and I have called it a night and agreed to meet for breakfast, I catch Amlan at Bandra Bandstand for paper cup coffee and cigarettes. Sitting on the wall, with Shah Rukh Khan's mansion behind us, I tell him about Dhruv. He considers the situation carefully.

'Better watch out, boss. He sounds like a full-on GMPT to me.'

'A what, dude?'

'Oh, you've never heard of a GMPT? Maybe it's a Bombay thing.'

Of course it's a Bombay thing. If Bombaywallahs were to have their way, *bread* would be a Bombay thing. The rest of us in the provinces would eat stale rice all year and dream about that one time in Colaba we had *bread*.

'Stop being random. What's a GMPT?'

Amlan relishes this. He stands up, lodges his fag in the corner of his mouth and frees up his hands for grand gestures.

'A GMPT is what we in Bombay call a Ginsu Master of Positional Thinking. I keep forgetting you work inland and don't know these things. See, because this man is a Ginsu Master of Positional Thinking, he can take you in any position. If he's your senior, he'll be on top. If he is your junior, he'll screw you from below. If he's behind you, oil your ass, and if he's facing you, you're going to be gagging. The true GMPT knows more ways to fuck your happiness than you know to orient yourself.'

'Ok. I'll be careful. But maybe getting fucked over is also a Bombay thing? Then I only need to worry when I'm here, right?'

But, you know, Amlan's bitching and dissatisfaction is part of the game, the fancy hotels, big cars, the shiny expense account. We all bitch. It's a reflex. But it's all worth it when the moment of magic comes. When the money hits my account at the end of the month and my bank sends me the text alert, for a moment, I am lost in the digits. I can look at the world with a fresh pair of eyes. Every item I see gets divided into one of three categories: 1) affordable, 2) forever unaffordable or 3) affordable on instalment if I keep this rate of earning up. That's right, in our old patois, I'm a Big Man now.

All in all, I suppose things got messy towards the end, but they seem to have sorted themselves out okay. I can't say it's going badly at all. In fact, I could even go as far as to say I'm contented, for the first time in a long time

But I remember what Sasha had to say about that. Four years ago, I was lying in bed in a pair of shorts reading a book. I looked up to see him smoking a fag and looking down at me. I returned to my book, then looked back at him. He was still looking at me thoughtfully. I decided two could play at this game and returned to the book. The next thing I felt was a searing burning pain as Sasha ground out his cigarette in my belly button.

More than anger, I felt bewilderment.

'You bastard,' I yelped as I scratched at the butt and the blistering flesh around it. 'Why would you do that?'

'Because you look too happy,' Sasha said, 'and contentment is the worst enemy a man like you can have.'

just what i needed

The Cars/The Cars/1978

Now that it's over for good, maybe I can place what it was I loved about Jennifer and why it happened in the first place.

It was my birthday and she had called to wish me. I was drunk and I wanted to take a long punt. It's an ancient Indian disease – see the Mahabharata for perspective.

So I picked up the phone, heard her delightfully accented voice wishing me and, balancing myself against a bike in the parking lot, I heard myself step into the boots of the guy I wanted to be – self assured, confident, pulling them on, pulling the laces up.

'Well, you know what would make it happier?'

'What, Zorawar?'

'If you'd come to Pecos for lunch tomorrow.'

Seconds passed. Angels grew wings. Mandalas turned. I held my breath.

'Sure.'

I must have continued with the Big Man act until she hung up and then passed out with a smile on my face. I woke up at dawn on the terrace, mosquito bitten and tetchy from sleeping on a stone slab all night.

The next day at Pecos, across a cold pitcher and spicy pork curry with dosas, I found myself talking endlessly, and it was all big-mouth bullshit, but her eyes encouraged it. How much her eyes had to do with it, beautiful eyes like almonds, brown and warm like bushes. Almonds set in the face of a sculpture, perfectly symmetrical, down to the fine point of her chin, surrounded by bouncing hair, a face that could be twenty or fifty or immortal.

When we walked across the street in the late afternoon sunlight, head spinning slightly, into the old second-hand book paradise where the century had never turned, and we sat on a stool and she leaned her back against mine, I was sold. That touch of vertebrae aligned our stars.

Which is why the long way in was so pleasant. The coffee at the India Coffee House under the gaze of the starched and turbaned old staff; the night at the Kryptos show when I nearly kissed her, but she turned her head and I had to pretend I was reaching for my drink; the oddity of the walk to Five Buck Shop, knowing that people saw us together and we didn't know what this was either.

So when we finally became something together, it should have felt inevitable – the maturity of an investment. It didn't.

We were going to some gig in a school ground in central Bangalore. She wanted to head to town early for something, which I thought would be shopping. Stepping from the auto at Commercial Street, she walked quickly.

'Follow me.'

I followed, through crowds, piles of garments, hawkers and vendors till, many turns later, I was in an old gali, still following, but on the sides were temples and old jewellery stores. She stopped.

'Zoju. I want to get my belly button pierced. Can you stand the sight of blood?'

'I can try.'

Up until that point, I had never seen anything pierced. It was something I thought women did at an early age. She sat in a chair and the old silversmith cut a length of wire with his pliers, it's virginal point gleaming bright. He swabbed down Jennifer's belly, which I saw for the first time, the soft rounded muscle. Taking my hand, she nodded and he, with his thin practiced fingers, pushed it through the skin on the inside of her belly button, paused as she gasped, and pushed it through and out. The promised blood trickled forth and down to her belt. Then with an alcohol swab and a quick twist, it was done.

This is the kind of thinking I don't do anymore. I'd like to, but the choices don't even show up anymore. Something about seeing the metal enter Jennifer's skin pushed me over the edge. 'I want one,' I said, 'I want a piercing.'

Two minutes later, my ear throbbing and red, we left laughing and holding hands, delirious with the joy of our shiny new metal. The chemical triggers in my head fired and I no longer felt like waiting. I reached down and straightened her mouth. Reading the assent in her eyes, I kissed her for the first time, in that old empire of stone and gems. The world crumpled and compacted around us like snow in a fist.

Now spring is here again. I wonder, is Jennifer walking trails with someone new? Is she on a beach, walking out of the sea, her skin encrusted with salts? Is she in a city, like me, ignoring the turning season?

I remember one smell above all, a single nose tickle to designate the season. Spring is the smell of the bushes on the trail we once walked on the Western Ghats. On the curve of the hill, we stopped at some rocks covered with a spreading tree and took a nap that cost us an hour of daylight. An hour with her head in my lap, with the softness of the shawl her mother had given her under us, and the smell of her skin and the dry grass intermingling, each struggling to rise above the other, her skin winning ultimately, as I, unfair referee, came closer to it. What skin it was, luminous, taut like a grape. When she opened her eyes, I wanted to shut them to make sure the light within wouldn't leach out.

That night, probably due to the hour of daylight we squandered, when the sun melted into a reduction of red paste across the ranges, we were still on the trail, with no sense of the distance we had ahead. We walked ahead because we knew there was no way to track back, till the road turned to path and the path to trail. Holding hands, stumbling over roots in the dark, we came upon the stones of some dead civilization. An old temple in the dark, with moss on its large granite blocks and, behind it, a step well.

Following the steps up from the well's black waters, up the curve of the hill, we found a trail leading up the slope, stepped from the same stone by the fiat of those rulers and the wisdom of their dead architects. We have history to spare in this country. We have history to burn and tear down in the name of gods and casuistry, and we have history to flog to foreigners and, when we're done with all that, we still have enough history to guide young lovers in the dark. That path of cracked steps led us to shelter that night, to a light winking through the trees, and ultimately to a squat hill mansion, left behind by one of the British governors of India. A suspicious night guard, with his head wrapped up in a scarf, peeked out at us when we knocked. Seeing us, his heart softened. He let us in and let us have a storeroom with a single cot and a basin in the corner, the white paint flaking off the wall.

I don't think that Jennifer, even with whatever hatred she may bear me now, could have forgotten that night in the mansion of the old governor. I read to her from my tattered streetside edition of *The Prophet*, and every word rang true and reverberated in the room and in my head, and I felt like weeping at its truth. In between the chapters, we made love, reading and holding each other till dawn. What love we made – like stars colliding, like the tension of violin strings, like the cries of every living thing, we shrank the world to the inside of that one white room for those hours. In the middle of the night, we stepped out, she wearing the shawl and I nothing, and marvelled at the stars and the silence. We were above the mist and the world below was invisible; the night above radiant. When, in the morning, we woke and headed down, back to buses and traffic and functioning phones and the twenty-first century, her heart was mine.

ain't no easy way

Black Rebel Motorcycle Club/Howl/2005

As I clean my football boots off after the game this morning, I realize that it has become a habit. I've been doing this since second year. First, I wipe them down with warm water, then I put a smidgen of oil on them to really take off the ingrained dirt. When I'm done, they gleam with menace. My tools are clean and I put them away with a final rub of the cloth.

It's the sort of habit great players rarely develop because the respect an artist has for his tools can never approach the adoration a mere workman has for them. It was an uphill task for me to become a functional footballer, and it was always clear that I could never be the kind of player that Sasha and Raghav were, whose feet were all the insurance they needed in any situation. I had to learn the things they never had to think about.

Breaking into the university team meant everything to me. It was also a function of era, I suppose. The early 2000s really saw the renaissance of the defensive midfielder. Not since Franz Beckenbauer had the position mattered so much. With Genaro Gattuso at Milan, Claude Makalele at Madrid and Patrick Viera at Arsenal, sometimes it seemed that championships were merely a function of who you had shielding the defence. Until then, at least in our lifetimes, it had seemed a bit of a tactical afterthought.

I invented myself as that kind of player, running extra laps in the afternoon, doing squats and lunges to build up leg strength. We can't all be Zidanes, after all, touched by the divine trace. What I would never have in grace or vision, I could try to make up in viciousness and sheer bloody-mindedness. I'd run my laps, shine my boots and wait. I waited my way to our class team. The next year, I made it to the bench of the university team. And by fourth year, there really weren't any seniors left and the juniors were all turning up tails, so I became the starting defensive midfielder.

The joy I felt running out in an NLS shirt was wholly out of proportion to the standard of football we played. We were a great Law School team, really, a superbly conditioned and skilled Law School team, but as far as college football teams go, we sucked even on the almighty pooper of Bangalore football. We could beat medical teams – sometimes. But against any quality opposition, that is, any actual undergraduate institution with a sports quota, we'd get rogered. If we managed to hold a powerhouse like Al Ameen to a draw, we went out and celebrated. If we opened up our offence enough to actually score a goal, they would score four.

It's not that we lacked skill – our best players were skilful enough. But what do you say about a footy team that needs cigarettes at half-time? We practised together maybe once a month, just before a tournament. Our ground looked like a slice of war-torn Afghanistan. It even had a little island of bushes and reeds at the centre circle. We weren't the kind of team that did well competitively. But when we took buses across town to play some team, we believed. We had strategies that ignored basic things, that our central midfielder had cut to Goa for the weekend, or that our wingers didn't know how to cross the ball in. We just may have been the most cerebral team in India. In fact, we could probably have taken on equivalently intellectual football superpowers anywhere – like the Caltech Faculty team, or the Sunday squad at the Sorbonne's Art School. Unfortunately, football has a nasty habit of being played on the ground.

On our way back from defeats, there would be raging arguments about whose fault everything was.

Sasha said, 'Listen, I really should be playing midfield. I can link up with Raghav better than anyone else and we'd get forward more.'

Kelkar was woeful. 'We conceded four goals. I doubt we can lose you in defence.'

Raghav snorted, 'You conceded three of those all by yourself, mate. Sasha might as well have been in midfield.'

Regardless of the game he had, Kelkar wasn't going to take shit from Raghav. 'Listen, *mate*, if you ran ten feet in any given direction, we'd stop losing passes in midfield. Since you don't, *mate*, all of Zoju's passes to you get intercepted, we never cross the halfway line, and Sasha and I are facing an attack every minute.'

'Zoju would misplace passes no matter where I am. He enjoys passing to the other team.'

I had been quiet, pretending I wasn't really there. All the passes I had misplaced were coming back to me, an inverse highlight reel. What use was a defensive midfielder who couldn't make safe passes?

'What do I do?' I came back now. 'If I pass back to Sasha or Kelkar, Sasha yells at me and tells me to get it out forward.'

'Well, if you could dribble just one man and not be so fixated on getting rid of the ball, we wouldn't keep getting fucked at the back.' Sasha's face was red and his hands were up, fingers elongated in anguish. 'Why are you so afraid of straying more than ten feet out of the box? You couldn't possibly cost us more possession than you already do. Which is not to say that,' he said, turning to Raghav, 'you shouldn't track back a little to help us build the game forward.'

'What do I do, man,' Raghav would say defensively, 'you know I'm playing on a weak ankle. There's only so much I can run back if I'm ever supposed to pass forward.'

And so it would go on. We all knew each other so well that we'd take aim straight at the insecurities and let each other have it, pulling no punches. Sasha could be petty and vindictive and mean, like a cornered snake. He would hit out at the smallest weaknesses, the unnameable shortcomings. By the time the bus got back to campus, Amlan would be sitting at Five Buck Shop, marinating in ill-disguised glee.

'So, you've gone and covered yourselves in glory again, huh?'

'Go fuck yourself.'

Amlan would exhale smoke joyously. Criticism and insults were like candy to him. 'I don't know why you guys haven't given up yet. If you had this kind of success rate at business, you'd be bankrupt by now.'

Of course, it was never about winning or losing. Playing football was about that one transcendental moment that every player knows, the unanticipated holy instant. For ninety minutes, the Arsenal offence keeps crashing, wave after wave of forward runs, all breaking on walls of stolid defence, and then there is just one breathtaking moment of clarity when Fabregas misdirects the whole defence with a magician's handkerchief and plays someone in with a through ball. There's silence as van Persie collects the ball in the box and you know that there is no way that he can *not* score because this is a moment of magic. Then the waves of noise crash down again – it's only a football match – but the after-image stays, of an instant when everything stood still for a second of genius.

The heart of all magic is that transformation, creation and second sight. In the golden age of Victorian magic, the magician would drop powdered phosphorous on a candle. In that flash, the rabbit would disappear, the padlocks would click open and time itself would stand still for the venerable moustachioed craftsman to perform his sleight.

Back when we whiled away the sunshine sitting on slabs of concrete, pouring the minutes through our fingers, there was always that sense that great things were around the corner, that the next bus that showed up would take us somewhere magical. You'd be walking a lousy, grimy path and the world's greatest little teashop would jump out of nowhere. When you opened your door and stepped out, anything seemed possible.

Sometime over the last year, and I can't put my finger on exactly where, I have lost the ability to believe in magic.

The static has risen and overwhelmed everything and I am drowning in the noise, trying to make sure I don't swim straight down.

We were the first generation of Indians for whom football was the biggest sport in the world, for whom cricket was the *other* sport. With us, this newly alien faith took root. When the Premier League came to India, we were finishing school, and already had the fever when we came to college. I had never even kicked a ball in anger. So when I was watching, I was learning the sport at an entirely cerebral level. I knew what a slide rule pass was before I learnt that you don't kick the ball with the toe of your boot.

Is this really the same Arsenal we used to watch together in the common room, sitting on folding metal chairs, under a slowly revolving fan with the sounds of ping-pong balls being punished in the background? Invincible Arsenal, the Arsenal of Dennis Bergkamp and Patrick Viera and Thierry Henry? I remember the first Arsenal game I watched, in second year. It was like watching the Assyrians fall on a farming settlement, wolves upon the fold, the English sunlight coming down on Freddie Ljungberg pacing down the side.

'Look at that,' I would point. 'Viera. That's class. He goes in, comes out with the ball, makes the simple pass and people forget about him. He's so good and utterly forgettable. He's the most indispensable member of the team.'

'Yeah, but you can't make a team of ten Vieras. Where's your inspiration going to come from? You need Bergkamp more, because a player like that comes along once a decade.'

'Inspiration is all well and good, but football is not about everyone scoring goals all the time. You have to marry occasional inspiration with constant containment. Bergkamp is a luxury on an already great team.'

Sasha shook his head sadly. 'That's the recipe for successful, ugly football.'

'Football at that level is about winning, Sasha. There's no room for pretty passing unless it's risk free.'

'Zoju, listen, they don't call football the beautiful game because of its intrinsic properties.'

'Of course they do.'

'No. All sports are equally beautiful. There's nothing more beautiful about the way football is structured or the number of players or the size of the field. It's not meant from the perspective of the viewer at all. The reason it's the beautiful game is because it's so much fun to kick a ball on the grass and go run after it. It's an *interior* beauty.'

'That's fine for you and me to say, but it's not true when it actually matters, on the ground.'

Sasha sat up, his fingers spreading in anguish. 'No! Don't you understand that it's most important to play beautifully when it really matters? Winners come and go, but you don't remember anyone for lifting a cup. The teams that stay with you are the ones who took the risks and chose to play beautifully. Think about Holland in 1974 or Brazil in 1982. They both lost to far uglier teams, but there's no way you could name as many players on the winning team as you could on the losing side.'

'Those *were* winning teams, Sasha. They only lost the last match of the tournament. Arsenal are only beautiful because they're winning. If they were playing like this without Viera, and were conceding as many goals as they scored, they'd be ugly.'

'No, Zoju, it's bigger than that. It's about how you look at life. What prize do you get at the end of life? None. You'll die. I'll die. We all will. But some of us will be remembered for trying to get it right.'

When I think about it, I see the dusk mingling with the dust rising off our field. The sky was orange-purple and the white of cotton. Every evening, I'd watch all of us impose our personalities on the game as best as we could.

I was a momentum player. When things were good, when I had time on the ball, when passes were pinging about smoothly, a confidence and faith would build up in me and then I would be crisp and strong like I wanted to be. When the tide turned, or the pressure was too great and passes were being intercepted, that sense of faith would wilt and wither. Sometimes I would just feel the ball pass me by and be unable to chase and harass and win it back. Or I would pass the ball, knowing even before I had made contact with it that I had actually passed it away and lost possession. Something inconsistent and weak in me would rise up and throttle me. In the same way, when things weren't working, I'd let courses pass me by, let moots and essay contests pass me by. You can drift through games, you can drift through years, you can drift through life and I drifted through the lot of them.

Kelkar, on the other hand, was dogged, never letting his technical deficiencies hold him back from putting his limbs and those of others at risk – the same way he would stay up all night for weeks writing projects like they were groundbreaking treatises. If he was bypassed, he would run so hard that even the rock hard soil bore stud marks, catch up and get the ball back, by means fair or foul. You could try to complain, after you picked yourself up and caught your breath.

'What the fuck, man? Why do you always come in so hard, and with your studs up, always with your studs up?'

'Got the ball first.'

'Yeah, but we're practising. You'll hurt someone like that. You were at least a foot off the ground!'

'It's a man's game. And I got the ball. If you can't take the contact, don't come to play.'

'Just save it for matches, will you? And a proper pitch.'

'It's the same game on every pitch. And I don't see what you're complaining about. I got the ball.'

Sasha was just classes above us all. He was effortless, like an animal born to play football. His balance was immaculate. His positioning was perfect. When he was harrying for the ball, he would ruck up his shorts and snarl and dart sideways, eating up space. When he finally committed to the challenge, there was a subconscious calculus that was never wrong. He'd come away with the ball and dribble it out of defence, almost foolishly confident in his ability to find safe passage. Though he played at centreback, he always wanted to take free kicks. I can still see some of them, watching from behind the ball. He would run up with both arms out for balance, plant his anchor foot six inches from the ball, like all the good books say, and put the rest of his body through it and the ball would curve and dip magically. Sasha was exactly as good as he wanted to be.

Sometimes I thought he could be better, because he didn't really work on his game. There were evenings when I'd head out of the door and he wouldn't come because he wanted to sleep and read, or he wanted to think about a project. Those who have talent given to them, the way Sasha had it, rarely respect the work the average have to put in to get to the same level.

Raghav, for instance, because he didn't work at it, his injuries got the better of him until he was rarely match-fit. As the years passed, he played less and less, and played smaller and smaller parts in the games that he showed up for. Both success and failure are beasts that feed on themselves. If Raghav had been playing well and fit, he'd have gotten better and more skilful and more optimistic. He might even have stopped smoking joints on the sidelines with his shades on and warmed up instead. Running on that hellish pitch, I used to look at him and wonder if he knew how tempting he must have looked to the kids, the juniors who didn't want to run or practice or work, but wanted to play. He knew, of course he knew, the smile on his face, the blank reflection of his shades, the bounce of his hair, he knew how he was leading them all to worship luxury players, to care only for indolence and style.

Now, Raghav never plays. He is stuck at work and, when he's not working, he parties hard, then there's more work. Maybe some days he watches television and remembers when he could do a Zidane roulette and accelerate smoothly through a defence. I still get out of bed on weekend mornings if I'm not going to work and go play the five-a-side with the office lot; a bunch of old guys playing for an hour till they get knackered. I've invested too much work into the game to stop playing if I can. So I get out of bed on Sunday and hold my head in my hands and gingerly listen to the alcohol sloshing around inside and gauge whether I'll have to throw up or not if I were to go to play.

What forces me out of bed is the memory of the physical sensation of playing well. You make a couple of snappy sure passes, a clean well-timed tackle and the feeling takes over. The surge of confidence sneaks into your heart, your sweat stings warmly. Every muscle is moving independently, shouting out its existence, filling with the blood you're pumping into every extremity. Your shoes and shin guards are tight like armour; the hair stands alert off your scalp. The feeling of a volley clearance; the striking surface of your foot catching the ball on the drop, the moment of inertia, where one force extends the other, and the ball disappears up into the sun, and drops out a second later like a coin descending from heaven. The mathematical moment when a pass finds a running player. The feeling of falling onto the wet, dewy green grass with its musk of fertile earth and the tingle of the blades across your eyelids as you roll over to absorb the impact. The feeling only fades when you step off the pitch and sit down and feel the fatigue hit, the strain in your ankle, the pull in your hamstring as it cools down. The catcalls of your age and mortality bother you.

That will never happen to Sasha. His golden limbs will never rust. He will always be twenty-two years old, his body firm and his eye true, always able to measure up the arc of a final ball. In a way, Sasha will never come off the green pitch, will never cool down, never tire. There's no bitter bench for him, no ice bath or warm massage, no post-game drink, no lesser pleasure, only the affirmative moment.

That is the reason I'm angry at myself when I let the little things go; when I lose possession in the final third of the ·itch. It's because I finally realize how lucky we are to still be on this green planet, under the bright sun, with the use of our limbs, however rusted and uneasy their movement may be. How lucky we are to be able to kick a football and run after it. Not caring enough is not a crime against a club or its fans or an insult to the shirt. It's an affront to the incapacitated, the infirm and the dead.

today

The Smashing Pumpkins/Siamese Dream/1993

When they first started distilling liquor and putting it in barrels to age, a few hundred years ago, they discovered something inexplicable. They would put a certain amount of liquor in a barrel and put it away for a few years, and when they emptied it out, there was a discernibly smaller amount. After they were done suspecting the servants, they thought that maybe the wood had soaked it up. But the wood was as dry as any barrel could be and, when they tasted it, they found that though it was a little weaker, the flavours were sweeter and richer and more complex.

In truth, the alcohols had partially evaporated through the pores in the wood, leaving behind the heavier particles, which carry flavour in greater concentration. Because this wasn't readily apparent back then, they just accounted for the lost volume under a supernatural head. They called what they had lost the angel's share. They believed that an angel would take a little of their drink and, in exchange, ss the rest of it with celestial flavour.

When the spirit was raw, before it leached flavour from the barrel, and gave some of its potency to the angels, when things were good, in those years in the beginning, our lives were unspeakably beautiful.

If I met Jennifer instead of late afternoon footer, and we took a walk, sometimes, we would walk up to the hill. The trees would give way to stepped rocks, rocks out of a Mantegna, massive and engrossing slabs of earthbone peeking through the undergrowth. Under the eucalyptus trees, with their sharp blade-like leaves, their china white trunks headed for the sky, we would make love, intoxicated by the tickle of the grass and the weeds and little thistles, the sun that shone in late afternoon force. Like the gods intended, sweating and whispering in the dry grass, her nipples like berries, her hair like dark straw. As the sky grew darker, the grey clouds pulling themselves like a mantle over everything, we dressed and made our way down, past the old buffalo, past the chai hut where Amma watched knowingly, adding sugar to the tea she kept boiling on her gas stove and to Nagarbhavi for a cigarette and the search for drinking company for the night.

The most common setting for the lost hours of our lost lives was Surya, up the street from college. No plans were necessary, because everyone you liked was there anyway.

The secret to Surya's success as Law School's second home was the minimalism of the set-up. A crumbling concrete staircase led up to a dimly lit large room always full of men ordering hard liquor by the bottle. When a woman entered, all eyes turned to her; the modest South Indian woman does not ever enter an establishment like Surya, except to scrape her miscreant husband off the tiles.

But we didn't drink in there unless it was raining. The same staircase turned and led up to the roof, a flat slab whose concrete is broken only by iron rods jutting out at intervals and a small structure at the end, which serves as storage. The modus operandi was that you turned up and sat on the floor and tried to flag down the midget waiter who would then take your order and bring it to you in no particular order. Everyone sat on the slab in circles with the people they wanted to, and people circulated between circles, and as the night went on, there would be more mingling, until the last few groups of people all coalesced and walked back together. Relationships started and ended there. Feuds intensified and dissolved. Friendships got deeper. Secrets were entrusted and revealed.

You could order almost any sort of IMFL in Surya, but really the only drink that mattered was Old Monk rum. A quarter of Old Monk required a brace of Thums Ups and a dash of lime. The well-worn line was that the Old Monk was the only truly religious person anyone knew.

On the Surya terrace, with a shawl wrapped around us, with me drinking the Monk and Jenn putting away vodka and Sprite, we fit into the universe like pieces of a puzzle. Raghav would be with us or Sasha or sometimes Kelkar. Raghav and Kelkar would never be there at the same time.

When we'd finish and head down the street, always drunk enough to consider it rolling rather than walking, we'd have separated, talking to whichever friend from whatever group at Surya, just in time to make the gates shutting.

From there, I'd head up to the terrace for a late-night ke session. The purple night on the terrace, with the trees swaying in the wind, the stars clear and bright. The cherry on the joint would glow brighter as it went around the circle, and someone would be rolling another.

It is no sin to have forgotten yesterday. It is as if the slab of concrete is a slice of reality levitating above the terrace. There is community now between all who inhabit this concrete world. This is cheap magic, and common, and all who smoke connect to the same everyday miracle.

'It's the worst school ever,' groaned Seshadri, lying back on the slab. 'I can't believe I went there for six years.'

'Who else?' asked Kelkar, who had just taken the short run up to the edge of the terrace and sent an empty quart bottle spinning out into the night sky, to land in the trees behind the hostel. No one had ever been there, but everyone had a mental image of a carpet of broken and unbroken bottles, and the occasional corpse of someone who made the terrible mistake of sneaking out there after dark.

'Ummm ... Abhay, Rohit, Deepika, Shomu, Chiru, Aabha, Samyaka, Tanmay ...'

Kiran let out a laugh. 'That's not a school, boss. It's a catchment area.'

'I know. Thirty thousand people in one branch. Like a small town.'

Amlan liked to bring up the relevant material, marshalling the best and most persuasive evidence. He cued up the clip on his phone yet again, the familiar rustles and pleas filled the air. 'At least you got decent basic sex education.'

Seshadri laughed, 'Yeah, all the commerce chicks,' and then he spanked his knee with vigour, 'all the commerce chicks. There's nothing like a slutty commerce chick in a white shirt playing basketball on a humid July afternoon. I swear those girls sweat on purpose. They had no interest in playing the game, it was just a giant teasing session.'

Kiran struggled to the surface of his drunkenness, 'Oh man, you should have seen the girls at St Mary's in Allahabad play. Very different uniform. They had this pinafore. Most erotic pinafore in the history of pinafores. Basically a long banian with no sleeves, no belt, went down to mid thigh ...'

Kelkar doubled over with laughter. 'You guys should hear yourself. There's so much tension built up, you've got cum bursting out of your ears.'

Seshadri said, 'But we're all like that. It's the condition of the Indian male till college.'

A bitter laugh from Amlan. 'Yeah, and then what happens? The flowering and fruition of everybody's sex life? The only one who's come up with any bright ideas yet is Zoju.'

Kelkar puts his knife in. 'That's because Zoju is a Big Man.'

'A Great Man.'

'A Great and Powerful Man.'

I dimly perceive that I am being laughed at and struggle to come back. The best way of doing this is to target a newcomer. Raghav hoved into view from around the corner. 'There's your truly Great Man. All my achievements pale before his.'

'What's going on? Anything left to drink?'

'Nope. Now we're drunk and talking about chicks. Feel free to share your thoughts, any tips or advice you may have, Great and Powerful Man.'

'Fine. The easiest way to get laid is to be funny. Once she's laughing, it's easy.'

'There you go, boys,' Seshadri sums up. 'Raghav Sir's Top Tip Number One – Laughter is a lubricant.'

Women of the World, if you want Energizer bunny love, may I put forth as a candidate the middle class Indian male, aged eighteen. Is hard enough to put a nail through a brick wall, never runs out of bullets, never says no, never has emotional issues, will run a hundred miles through quicksand for it. And there's endless variety! Hallelujah!

Because we drank too fast and too much, it would hit us late and hard, and the latter part of every night is blacked out of my memory. As a result, I have no memories of ever coming down, only the blurred upward vector to oblivion, then waking up in strange rooms, on terraces, on steps and piecing the night together, explaining to yourself the scrapes on your lower back, the traffic cone in the centre of your room.

I stretched, the blanket sloughing off my arms, and slowly opened my eyes, wiping away the crust from them with my thumb and forefinger, already aware of the sweet smell of ganja and the strain of Eddie Van Halen's guitar. My feet felt the subwoofer shake the floor as the chorus of Eruption took hold again.

Sasha's taste drove me up the wall sometimes. The Beatles and The Who were old friends, but the idolization of Van Halen and Kiss I was not prepared to stomach. Sasha would calmly and infuriatingly argue that I actually agreed with him and only disagreed for the sake of argument. As a trick it was flawless; forcing the substance of any argument *in limine*. I raved and ranted and raised the question of burden of proof. Mere procedure and pathetic trickery, Sasha said, because it was a universal truth that Kiss was Great Music. I would be rendered speechless and forced to exit the room. A victorious Sasha would strip down to his shorts and prance around to 'Panama' or 'Cold Gin'.

I reached out for my water bottle. It wasn't there. Of course it wasn't. Sasha had obviously bonged it in the twenty minutes he had been awake. Over the last few months, I had given up on the possibility of owning a plastic bottle for more than a few hours at a time. You would think it was an easy dream to fulfil, and it was. Except around Sasha. Within hours of straying into his vicinity, any water bottle would be made into a water-bong, by the simple expedient of his cutting two holes in it and jamming the barrel of a pen into one. God forbid you wanted to drink water, or take notes, you would be out of luck, but you were never more than a minute away from a water-bong. Remonstrating with Sasha was an exercise in futility.

'Dude, where's my water bottle?'

'It's right here. Catch.'

'It has holes in it and looks dirty.'

'Oh that. I must have bonged it.'

'No shit. Why can't you just ask me, please, just once before taking the one bottle I own?'

Sasha would stand up and sing, wildly off pitch, 'Because Mama was queen of the Mambo, Papa was king of the Congo, deep down in the jungle, I start banging on my Bongo.'

'Please stop. Stop anywhere.'

He'd keep going. 'Now I'm the ... King of the Bongo, king of the Bongo, king of the Bongo-Bong! King of the Bongo, king of the Bongo, king of the Bongo-Bong!'

This morning, however, Sasha handed me the bong and I inhaled gratefully, sitting up in bed. Sasha moved to the shelf and lit an agarbatti to stick in the door. The sun streamed in through the window, lighting up the red of my blanket and the pile of clothes on the floor. Framed by the window was the huge gulmohur outside, with its flowers like tongues of flame, and a rusted metal chair stuck deep in its branches. We had long gotten rid of the curtains that separated our cubies, opening the room up. There was a central table with a hookah on it. One of the bookshelves held the remnants of an attempt to maintain a bar; all the bottles in it were empty. The floor had a friendly red rug askew in the centre. There were posters of Thierry Henry and Paolo Maldini up on the wall. I watched the smoke drift from my lips up to the slowly revolving fan where it was cut into nothing. I was wide awake and didn't feel like going anywhere, or doing anything, especially nothing related to class. Except eating. I was hungry.

'What's for breakfast?'

'Monday? White shit/Yellow shit.'

'Great. Did we do anything too retarded last night?' I asked, checking my phone's inbox, sent items and dialled numbers.

'Nothing out of the ordinary that I remember.'

'Good. No need to ask Kelkar.' Kelkar steered clear of the drugs, so there was usually at least one person around who had only been hammered on liquor the night before and could give you at least half the story. But he'd judge you for asking.

'What's first hour?' I asked, knowing that first hour was always Transfer of Property.

Sasha stopped his push-ups and said TP, and that he wasn't going.

'You're going to get yourself an attendance shortage, son.'

'Maybe. But I can't live with being the sort of asshole you are and the attendance you get by walking in forty minutes late.'

'I've gotten it up to two days late too.'

I put out the joint, which was done down to the roach, and threw it into the blue and white cup my mother had given me a year-and-a-half ago, which was an ashtray on the best of days. I threw aside the blanket altogether and stood up, pleasantly dazed. The music sounded like there were little speakers behind me, to my side as well as in the cubie opposite mine and like a lot more sustain was being used than I knew the song contained.

Sasha stood up behind me as I grabbed my towel and we both peered at the form in the hitherto undisturbed third cubie.

'What do you think will wake him up?' I asked.

'I don't know. Clearly, loud music is not the answer.'

'Poke him.'

'That's too déclassé.'

That was why Seshadri Ramachandran awoke on a glorious December morning with a feeling that his chest was hotter than it should be. Opening his eyes, he observed his roommates, with the care of a laboratory team, using a flamethrower improvised from his own deodorant and a lighter to singe his nipples.

'Bastards!'

Trusting that, in time, he would see the humour in the situation, I left the room for my bath, opening the door and releasing a wall of smoke into the corridor. A fifth year passed by and shook his head. 'Go to class, you dumbasses,' he growled.

Snagging a tube of toothpaste from the next room, I rolled to the bathroom in my towel, swinging my bucket. Sasha was waiting at the shower stalls, holding our dissolving cake of Lifebuoy – our room's one bar of soap.

'Zojeshwaran, let's take a shower together?'

'No, da. Have you noticed how I never say yes?'

'But you really should. It'll be so nice and fraternal.'

'It would be properly homo.'

'Of course not. We used to do this all the time at school. It's innocent and brotherly.'

I went into my own shower cubicle. Sasha could keep the soap. If I had to bathe with Rin, so be it. His voice came through the door.

'I'm using your tongue scraper. Is that okay?'

'No! You bastard!'

'Sorry. Done already.'

When we finally made it to class, I would try with varying levels of determination to stay awake. My head would drift back and then snap onto the base of my neck, waking me up. In seconds, my eyes would close slowly and my head would drift down till it made contact with my chest. I would jerk awake. The pattern continued until it was broken by a deep voice.

'Zorawar, if you insist on sleeping, you can do it in the comfort of your own bed.'

The urge to wake up kicked in deep in the spine. 'No, ma'am. Sorry. Won't happen again.'

'You know you're not sorry. I don't know what it is you spend all night doing, because it surely isn't studying history, but I will not tolerate you sleeping in this class. Next time, you will leave the class and lose attendance.'

The speaker was a short woman with severe features and her hair pulled into a tight braid at the back. She wore her white sari with a red border like a suit of armour. Ms K.R. Joseph was a history teacher, a feminist, a Marxist, and the terror of the first and second years. In addition to being a demanding teacher, she was the head of the examination department, which gave her the power to pass, fail or disqualify on the basis of insufficient attendance. Josie's interrogation was the most hair-raising thing a second year could imagine. The last thing I needed her to know was that I had spent most of the last night drinking and smoking the good leaf with Sasha. Especially with Sasha.

The Sasha–Josie equation was beyond comprehension. He succeeded, with the best intention in every case, to push each and every one of her buttons. She would invariably lose it and Sasha would have to leave the class and apologize later. When you asked him, 'Why do you fuck around with her so much, da?', he'd look astonished. 'She just picks on me, man.' So everyone paid attention every time Sasha raised his hand in class.

This time it was Kiran who swallowed the bait. Josie had put forth the proposition that feminists believe that modern technology was very much in the province of males. 'Look at even such a small indicator as the shape of spaceships. They're clearly all phallic symbols. It's obvious that the conquest of space is a gendered act.' Kiran put up his hand, his leg crossing over into the aisle and asked, 'Ma'am, how do you plan to send a donut-shaped ship into space?'

The question dropped into the calm bay of the class like a depth charge. There was silence as it sank in and then, the explosive sound of eighty people simultaneously choking back laughter. Some put their heads down and wept. Josie swelled up till she was bursting and then let rip, like a thunderstorm.

'Kiran, you are a disgrace to this institution and your parents, who I am sure are decent, hard-working people. You think you're so clever sitting in the back of the class making smart comments. If you only knew a tenth as much as the people you are so quick to criticize ...'

Kiran started to try and mitigate the damage he had caused. At this point, a hand in the fourth row went straight up. Sasha had something to say. 'Ma'am,' he said, in a reasoning tone of voice, 'why don't you just listen to him?'

Josie's head turned so fast you could hear her vertebrae snap in the back of the class. 'You will teach me manners, Sasha? YOU! You are the single-most ill-behaved lout I have seen in fifteen years of teaching here ...'

Sasha raised his hands above his head as if calling to the gods for justice. Then he banged the table hard with his fists and shouted, 'Ma'am, you could stand to learn manners from a five-year-old child! You pick on Kiran and you pick on me every single day. I am sick of it; the injustice,' he searched for the right word, sniffing his thumb with rage, 'it *irks* me. Raghav gets away with murder in this class.'

Raghav, who had, till then, been enjoying the showdown, with his mouth wide open, froze like a deer caught in the headlights. But the moment had already passed. Before the ugliness in the classroom could reach a conclusion, the bell rang. Josie stormed straight up the aisle to her room, and it was reported that there was a suspicious moisture in the dragon-lady's eye.

Later, in the common room, Seshadri glued to the wall a leftover prize certificate from the college fest. Raghav Gulati had taken a handsome first place in getting away with murder.

Seshadri was more interesting than anyone gave him credit for. He created much of his own image knowingly. His bookishness was genuine, but he needn't have dressed that way – his stiff starched cotton shirts always tucked into his pants. His glasses need not have had rims so thick. He could have purchased running shoes that weren't so relentlessly white. He could have topped the class without being such a terrific nerd. But he loved the role, the perverse bastard.

One afternoon, Kelkar was on the terrace, sunbathing face down on a Sunday morning, turning over alternately and rubbing lotion on himself. His skin had the warm reddish glow to it that comes to a brown man sunbathing. He yelled out to Seshadri, who lived below the terrace, to play him some Springsteen nice and loud so he could hear it on the terrace.

Seshadri was in a foul mood. Something in his project on mortgages wasn't working out. The theory of English land law had been adopted unevenly in Indian statutes and he was at a loss for exact equivalents. So he saw Kelkar out on the terrace, greasy and turning red, and his dirty little mind started turning.

Seshadri set him up so sweetly. He put 'Born to Run' on loop. He ensured Amlan and I came up, to create a sense of security, to pass the deed on to the public and to protect himself. Then he chatted Kelkar up. He talked to him about something stereotypically Seshadri, something boring like energy security or the situation in Darfur. You know, something that Seshadri would find interesting and wouldn't cause Kelkar to change the topic – unlike, say, the public distribution of foodgrain, something that could interest only Seshadri.

So he worked Kelkar, slowly lulling, almost singing him to sleep. Then, Seshadri kindly patted him on the back and stroked his famously luxuriant back hair. Rathore had once terrified him by threatening to wax him with a bedsheet and a pot of Fevicol.

With dexterity you wouldn't believe him capable of, Seshadri pulled a straight razor from his pocket, held it up to the sun like some Brahmastra from the Mahabharata and took exactly four quick swipes at Kelkar's back. Then, as Kelkar struggled to his feet, his eyes red with rage, Seshadri bowed with a flourish and ran as fast as his legs could carry him.

There on Kelkar's back, clearly visible as he stood up to give chase, was a perfectly symmetrical back hair butterfly. Can you believe that they nearly gave Seshadri a Rhodes scholarship?

When we weren't creating trouble for each other, trouble would come for us.

Kelkar came back from town one Friday feeling peakish and went to his room, drew the deep blue curtains and went to sleep. By evening he had a full-blown fever and a sore throat. He took two Crocins and went to sleep. He woke up early the next morning and went to the bathroom, feeling a little weak but alright to brush and shave. When he looked up at the mirror, what he saw surprised him. Around his mouth and neck were half a dozen areas of reddish swelling. Alarmed, he went to the doctor instead of going to class, figuring he could manage medical attendance make up.

Raghav was smoking at Five Buck Shop in the eleven o'clock break as Kelkar came down the street, clearing his throat.

'Oye, what's up? Why'd you skip two hours of Pol Ski?'

'Nothing much, yaar. Feeling like shit. Went to the doctor. Really odd.'

'So, what's wrong with you?' asked Raghav, who could not really have cared less.

'He says I have something called Herpes ... Gladiator? Gladiatoris?'

'You have herpes!'

'Yeah,' Kelkar laughed uneasily. 'Funny no? But it's a kind of herpes you get from the gym or playing sports. Wrestler's herpes, he called it.'

'Oh, right. Well, if you need something, just call.' Raghav skedaddled off to class and Kelkar went to his room to sleep off the throbbing in his head.

He woke up at two in the afternoon and Amlan was in his room, smoking a cigarette and leaning against the cupboard. Seeing his eyes open, Amlan pointed his cig at him and said, 'I don't judge you.'

'You what?'

'I said, I want you to know that I'm not judging you. I've thought about it and I'm different from everyone else.'

'Who what? Judging me?' Kelkar did not dig.

'It's okay. We all make mistakes. If our friends don't stand up for us, who will? I'm here for you, man.'

He shifted the cigarette to the corner of his mouth and used both his hands to hold Kelkar's arms gingerly above the T-shirt cuff, gazing meaningfully into his eyes.

'I love you, man, but you're never coming anywhere near my sister.'

Amlan turned and left before Kelkar had anything to say.

Kelkar crawled out of his bed and went looking for Raghav. However, in addition to the world's largest mouth, Raghav also possessed a low animal cunning and highly developed survival instinct. He had cut to town for the weekend.

Kelkar's troubles were to be greater than his sores and his maligned reputation. Exams started on Monday and there was no way he was going to be able to give them in the shape he was. So he went to Josie to ensure he could give the exams as first attempts next month. Her office was in the tower above the quad and he stated his suit at the door, for he did not dare enter.

'No, Ranjan! How can you even darken my door, with your sins all over your face, and ask for a first attempt?'

'Ma'am, I have a doctor's report here. It's a legitimate medical ground. The entire point of a first attempt is to give people who were involuntarily unable to take an exam a chance to take it without being penalized for their bad luck.'

'Ranjan, you will take the exam next month and it will be recorded as a repeat exam. First attempts are a discretionary measure for us to grant to deserving students who did not acquire STDs in god knows what back alley!'

'Ma'am! This is not an STD! The doctor says it's herpes gladiatora; it happens to sportspersons!'

Josie waved her hand at him dismissively. 'Really, Ranjan, who are you trying to fool? The only thing I don't understand is why you'd go off-campus for sex. We have lovely disease-free girls right here.'

She broke into her loud hollow laughter and Ranjan Kelkar, sick and light-headed from fever, beaten by powers bigger then him, proud and angry as one wronged, turned on his heel and walked out. If he had stayed, he might have argued further, called people, figured it out, but his mind was made up – he would suffer no more insults, whether he was to be debarred from winning gold medals or not. From that day onward, he had nothing to do with Josie. He wrote the repeats she made him write and passed them.

The unfortunate fallout was that Kelkar's slight dislike of Raghav become an enmity. What Raghav thought was harmless gossip-mongering had become treachery in Kelkar's eyes. Amlan and Kiran and I saw it play out before us every day. If Raghav entered a room, Kelkar would leave. Raghav would ask, 'What's up his ass, man?'

Kiran was disturbed by it, hated it, couldn't understand why his two friends couldn't get along. It was in Kiran's nature to hope that everything be ideal, that without a very good reason, two countries would never go to war, two guys would never dislike each other, the group, that unit of social existence, would never fall apart. Amlan saw conflict as the basic fact of life and enjoyed needling Kelkar about Raghav. Amlan had learnt very early in life basic truths about the need for all organisms to compete for a share of the eco-system.

Perhaps that was it. Two more different people were hard to find. Raghav was good-looking in a lean wolfish way; Kelkar was hunchbacked and stout, with a slightly receding hairline and crooked teeth. Raghav was good at lots of things without having to put much work into it: Kelkar got there with assiduous organization and work. Kelkar never had much to say to groups of people; Raghav would slip in easily like he was the paint on the wall. Kelkar grew to dislike the simple witty gloss Raghav gave to things, began to detest his drugs and the way he was slowly acquiring a set of friends whose life revolved around the taking of drugs, like Rathore.

Raghav, on the other hand, didn't think about Kelkar much. You can't disagree with a person more than that.

street fighting man

The Rolling Stones/Beggar's Banquet/1968

Out with it then: I am a coward.

Maybe it's my parents' fault, old Gandhians that they were. I was raised to believe it was wrong to fight and that you should always turn the other cheek. It used to feel noble when I was walking away from fights in the schoolyard, but somewhere along the way, it stopped being acceptable.

Somehow, every time I've gotten caught in a fight, I've been on the periphery of it. Always just getting the shit whacked out of me. When I should be feeling righteous anger, I just feel a cold dread deep down and icicles in the pit of my stomach. It would be much more acceptable had I not lived for five years with the bravest guy I've known.

One summer night in second year, the air as warm as it gets in Bangalore, cooling at night, Sasha and I had walked up to Surya to get our drink. On the way, as on a night when we meant business, we had stopped at the chemist for

Vitamin C and at the bakery for a bun-butter to line our stomachs. Then we ordered drinks and peanuts. Peanuts could be ordered as either Congress (salted and split into halves) or BJP (whole, but coated with a bright orange paste). We were feeling a little right of centre that night, so we got the orange ones.

Quart One came and went in a hurry, the night was young, the liquor well earned. It slipped down our throats like water, in minutes, without conversation.

Quart Two came like a blessing, the freedom of drink complete. Sasha and I together, his feet bare and facing upwards, mine elongated along the cold cement terrace of Surya. The lights of the street around us were dying. Sasha told me about how, when he had gone to Singapore, he had tried to force his way into the Star TV offices and offer his services to ESPN-Star as a sports analyst. There must be a shortage, he reasoned. 'After all, they let Shebbi Singh on air. Who the fuck is that guy?'

'He knows a little more than Steve McMahon, though.'

Sasha sat up and rubbed his face vigorously with his hands and then put on his best dour northern face by pushing his eyebrows up and rounding his mouth into an O. He looked nothing like Steve McMahon, and in fact looked even more the half-Nepalese he was. Then, through his strangely rounded lips, he pushed a tortured and mangled Irish comedy accent. There were dropped 'h's, there were dropped 'g's, there were superfluous 'r's and, needless to say, it sounded nothing like Steve McMahon.

'Staiven Gerrraahrd neeuds to put a whole lawt mawre cohmittmuhnt into fahlling buck and pickin' oop 'is mahn. Ah mean, this is Hanfield.'

'Excellent, really spot on, machan. Now do Stephen Appaiah.'

Appaiah was a player we both held in very high esteem and Sasha would go on for hours about how aristocratic he was with the ball, about how he was a natural leader, and in an earlier age he would undoubtedly have been at least a tribal leader, if not king.

Again, Sasha rubbed his face and reincarnated himself as Appaiah. Now his mouth split into as wide a smile as possible and his eyes narrowed till they were only slits. He crooned out, 'The Gana teeum ees gowing to be veyury prawmising at the next waorld caup. Theure are a lawt of exciting aoung plaayurs coming t'roo.'

Neither of us had ever heard Appaiah say a word, but I can give it to you on affidavit that that is not how he would speak. He sounded a lot like Steve McMahon, at least the way Sasha heard him. Sasha was a shit mimic.

Quart Three was the meat of the evening, the longest two drinks. It was also the most interrupted. Sasha went down to take a leak. I sat upstairs and drank slowly. I checked my messages and thought about projects and internships and, in my solemn drunken way, promised that the next day, I would go to the library and catch up on corporate law and civil procedure. Sasha came back up.

'You think you'll ever be a great lawyer, Zoju?'

'I don't know, da. Every time I intern somewhere, I think nobody knows much, but then when you see them work, they all just know so much.'

Sasha was contemplative. 'Well, I don't doubt that you could do alright at it, but do you think you could ever be great, like Seshadri will be great at it?'

'I frankly don't think I'll ever get it as well as Seshadri does. Do you think you could be great?'

'I don't know, man, Zoju. I don't know. But I know that I don't want to die unknown.'

There's really nowhere to go from a statement like that, so we repeated our order when the boy came back up.

Quart Four is always a mistake, but it is a solution to the mistake that would have been stopping at three quarts and going back down the street feeling so sober that it was a waste having gone drinking. We pushed through it, relishing the next day's hangover in advance.

Quart Five was just plain stupid. No two guys need a fifth quart but, if anyone was to blame, it's Quart Four. Quart Four ordered Quart Five.

I threw back the last of my drink and stood up reeling. I reached for the rod and straightened up. Suddenly, I realized that my bladder was full, begging for relief, but I couldn't bear the idea of going downstairs and negotiating my way through the mess of tables and drunks. Like I had hundreds of times before and as hundreds had before me, I headed to the edge of the terrace, unzipped, caught the washing line and pissed into the darkness, watching the traffic lights in the distance, moving slowly, decorously.

I heard a shout and a half-brick flew towards me. In the darkness not far from where I was filtering the better part of a bottle of rum, the wind had carried some of my product and wafted it over a couple of hangers-on. 'Motherfucker,' I screamed, enraged at the attempt on my cock, 'Go fuck yourselves.'

Just like that it was on. We came downstairs and they were waiting for us. The big guy was bald, bearded and wore a slug around his neck on a rubber necklace. He stepped forward, starting on what would have been an extended oration on the morality of his actions, like Krishna at Kurukshetra, no doubt. Sasha cut it short by running into him full tilt. Which left me to deal with the buddy, who was smaller than I am and wearing a greasy-looking leather jacket. I started by holding him off, telling him those two will sort it out. Next thing I knew, he'd punched me in the nose. I was bent over, holding it and feeling the nauseous mustard sting drain my brain, unstable, my feet giving up traction. Leatherjacket picked up a Coke crate. Suddenly I found myself being whaled with the crate, my face flat on the pavement. I just about got up and flung the crate away, noticing that Surya had already wound its shutters down.

Sasha and the big guy had already peeled out onto the street. As Leatherjacket went looking for his crate – I still hadn't touched him – Sasha grabbed the big guy and threw him over a car. In real life, not a movie, he threw him onto the roof of some ninja's Esteem and hard enough to come off the other side.

While I was gaping, Leatherjacket found a Coke bottle. Glass broke behind me – I turned and the guy missed my head and just scraped the top of my shoulder.

The sound of engines and wheels. The cops were here. Surya was shuttered, there was no way back in and Sasha and the big guy had separated. Leatherjacket was holding his bottle and there was blood on my shirt. There was no two ways to read this situation. The door of the patrol Gypsy opened and the cops with lathis piled out. Without a moment of hesitation, they turned on us, outsiders in their land, and chased us down the street while the big guy talked to the constable in Kannada. We scrambled in over the fence and got to safety as soon as possible.

We should have wisened up to the danger and xenophobia all around us as early as that, but we didn't. Our solution was to stop calling Kannadigas 'digas' on the principle that they would figure it out. So, from that day on, the natives of Karnataka became 'the Portuguese'. Often there was trouble with the Portuguese up at the circle, or Portuguese political rallies; people spoke Portuguese, Portuguese regionalism and militancy grew out of hand. We were just a colony of outsiders, in the heart of Portugal.

When people asked about the scar on my shoulder, I said I got it in a fight. But it wasn't the whole truth. The truth was that I got caught in a situation, reacted like a pussy, and got thwacked for it. In the same incident, Sasha got away with a light black eye and a ripped shirt. Fortune favours the brave and the rest of us get bottled from behind and take six stitches for our trouble.

If cowardice was my weakness, I was not alone. Jennifer's cowardice was her crippling lack of self-regard. It used to make me crazy angry – like when the chain on a bicycle has come free but you keep pedalling. I wanted to stuff her with sunshine, with the belief that she could do great things. One day she broke into some gospel thing while walking down the street with me.

'Jenn, you sing too well to not be doing it more seriously.'

'Flattery.'

'I don't need to flatter you. I'm already bonking you.'

She hit me playfully in the ribs with her little fist and then buried her face in my chest.

'Keep it up and you won't be.'

'Unlikely, you like my loving too much. But, listen, I'm serious. Why don't you get to town and find a voice coach, or get a band together and put some work into it?'

'I'm nowhere near good enough for that.'

'Of course you are! I'm telling you – I've heard you sing well and I've heard you sing badly, and you're better than anyone I've heard.'

Suddenly her face fell. 'I'm not, Zoju. Every second girl in Mizoram sings this well. There're a hundred girls on local radio better than me, and they aren't going anywhere. It's the only thing I'm good at and I'm not really very good at it.'

'You can give always give it a shot ... You can't win if you don't try.'

'I've tried, when I was a kid. Every Mizo girl tries it. Can't do it.'

In her own way, she was also a coward, so scared of failure that she never gave anything a clean shot. Even though she watched everything keenly, judging it, she never mooted or debated or tried to get onto any of the legal journals, because she couldn't bear to see her name below anyone else's. But the contempt she had for people! For Amlan, because he was fat. For Kelkar, because he tried too hard. For Malaika, because she got around. I wondered, if Jennifer did not love me, how many kinds of contempt would she have had for me? But no one else got to see the ambition inside her – that she thought she was better than everyone else, but they were trying and she wasn't. Only I got to see the queen in the cocoon.

There are days when you realize exactly how racist a country we are. Because being sectarian, casteist and class-conscious is not enough, we're also a country where being black or Northeastern means you live in a different world.

I think about Jennifer now and I realize how hard it must have been for her to have come all the way to NLS. If she hadn't made it, if she just pointed to the opportunities she didn't have, no one would blame her for laziness or lack of ambition. The harder thing would have been to come all the way and engage with the demons of this inequitable world. To then discover that she was intelligent and capable, but that, regardless, people would never treat her that way; the injustice would have cut away at her every day.

Maybe, and this is the most ridiculously refined kind of racism, I feel guiltier about the way things broke down with Jennifer because she was Northeastern. It's not easy being a Northeasterner in mainland India. People assume the worst of you. Maybe it goes back to the contempt a classical civilization has for the hinterlands, like the Greeks and their barbarians. But what's certain is the poisonous modern jealousy born of reservations, quotas and lists – that's when we care to think of the Northeast at all. We are raised to believe that people who get reservations get a free ride through life, that they never achieve because they never needed to and they reach plateaus for that reason and then their children benefit from it. But we are so insular a people, our ancient civilization so closed and narrow, so inward that we bar access to anyone outside so completely that actual equality will always be an illusion.

The ugly truth of our history is that the Indian nation, in its building, took the Northeast against its will. Everyone knows about Patel's skilled wrangling to get hold of Hyderabad and Kashmir and we admire him for it, the wily old bastard. What we don't discuss is that the Indian army went to Mizoram and found people they considered savages. And so the noble post-Vedic people sent the men to the fields to be guarded under guns, raped their women in the villages and then inducted them into our country. The honour was ours.

It gets better. We also suffer ghetto lust. The call of forbidden fruit, we desire their daughters and women. We desire their power and insouciance. We seek their coolness and fashion. If you're a good-looking Northeastern girl, every mainland Indian boy you know will eye you with lust for the exotic, but he will never take you home. Every mainland Indian girl will harbour doubts about your intelligence and your morals. Your worth in the world will depend on your hotness. How then can you be blamed for being insecure?

Lust was the key in which Raghav pursued targets. While the rest of us were happy getting any at all, Raghav was motivated by an almost childish desire to notch his bedpost. I call it a childish desire, because I was told it was a childish desire, and I am still told it is a childish desire, and yet it was – is – also my desire. What was black magic beyond Kelkar's reach or mine was child's play to Raghav. He knew how to strike up conversations with girls in clubs and bars and, more importantly, to convert attempts into goals. The rest of us were far less successful. On the rare occasions when Kelkar succeeded in carrying a conversation for a few minutes, he would make a pen pal. Sasha would end up saying something honest and rude and end the conversation. Amlan somehow was never interested. I would try my hand half-heartedly, feeling bound down and trapped by the fact that Jennifer and I had become, over time, a couple and I would resent the restriction. I would walk away, having ended the conversation myself. In the exact same circumstances, Raghav would find some way of leaving with his target and, while walking out the door, give us a wide smile and a triumphant middle finger.

So it was no surprise when, one night at Surya, he managed to hit home with Rohini. He had been building towards the point all evening. With single-minded concentration, from the late afternoon's first beer, with the sun going down over the urban sprawl of Nagarbhavi, to the coming on of the lights on all the buildings that hemmed in the Surya terrace and the switch to rum and Cokes, he chatted her up. He spoke a little, and he listened a whole lot more. Like an engineer directing the flow of a river, he channeled her into telling him more and more.

In the corner, Jennifer, I and Kelkar watched him.

'He's good,' Jennifer offered.

I shook my head. 'I don't know how he does it.'

'He's listening to her. That's all we women want.'

Kelkar could not tear his eyes away from them. 'What a con.'

'Ha! You'd kill to be where he's getting tonight.'

I wasn't even being facetious. Kelkar was madly in love with Rohini – from the first lecture on feminism she had given him in the quad. Not only was she sexy, sultry and heavy in all the right places, but she spoke passionately about legal reform and rights movements and transitional justice. She was a legal counsellor for battered women centres, someone who actually put her time where her mouth was. In addition, she was two years senior to us, and all Kelkar had ever wanted was something to put on a pedestal. Kelkar hated the fact that Raghav was even talking to her. I felt strangely jealous. The way you can feel jealous when you're holding a beautiful girl who's willing to have sex with you, but you're wondering if you have a shot with the girl across the terrace. At those moments, you feel something cloaked and misshapen glide into your heart, a dissatisfaction, a desire that is hard to describe. Once you let it in, there is no turning back; it will take up residence there and whisper sedition to you constantly.

At ten o'clock, Raghav paid the tab and left with Rohini. As he went down the steps, he turned and gave us a middle finger salute. Kelkar kicked a beer can all the way back to the hostel.

The next morning, Raghav came to class grinning. He had spent the night at Rathore's place with Rohini and, as he told me happily, 'Nailed and bailed, man, I didn't even have to deal with her in the morning.'

The reason became apparent the next day. Rohini filed a sexual harassment complaint with the college. Raghav received a summons in his hostel room. He went from stud to rapist in a blink; all the seniors stopped talking to him, girls looked at him with disdain, a walking ghost. Rohini became the victim. 'I never thought it could happen to me. I thought, no, I'm a strong vocal woman. How wrong could I have been!' she said, sitting in the quad, surrounded by girls in crushed cotton skirts and kajal.

The only friends Raghav had anymore were Sasha, Amlan and myself. But he preferred to retreat into the company of

Rathore, who offered him sanctuary in his house off campus, the scene of the crime. While the investigation and the hearing proceeded, Raghav moved in with Rathore and spent his time smoking weed and bitterly complaining about women who changed their minds in the morning.

Ultimately, Raghav took the case against him to court and the sexual harassment proceeding was tied up with a court stay. But the pattern was set. The authorities who ran NLS – the director, the faculty, Josie – saw us all in a set. Trouble had claimed us for its own.

death whispered a lullaby

Opeth/Damnation/2003

At dusk, the news had come to Five Buck Shop. We were sitting out in Nagarbhavi rush hour, watching people watch people, like a street of distrustful strangers in some spaghetti western. The fusillade of cigarettes sent off smoke signals that must have been visible to satellites. I was waiting for Amoeba, the man behind the counter, so known on account of the ease with which he grasps complicated concepts like 'Coke', 'Two Milds', or in this case, 'bun bhurji'. Amlan came panting up the slope and got hold of a cig. Then he released his brief.

'K.V. Nangappa is dead.'

This was news to us, as was the existence of the recently deceased in the first place (majority leader of the state legislature, apparently, who knew?), but the gathering immediately understood the unholy glee of the messenger. If somebody of sufficient importance kicked the bucket, we got a day off. On a Friday, this is good news. On the

Thursday of a week, in which Saturday is already a holiday, this is spectacular news, because we now have a three-day weekend and, by appending a Monday, a four-day weekend.

Suddenly, we were caught up in the whirlwind of a plan that had no centre and only arms, each one of which was throwing clothes into a bag. In went the toothbrush, sweatshirt, one T-shirt, socks, chuddies and a second-hand *Zen and the Art of Motorcycle Maintenance*. It was only when I ran to catch up with Amlan and Raghav that I got a real fix on where we were headed.

'Hey, you're coming, no?'

'Of course. But where am I coming?'

'Seshadri has a place in Kodaikanal. It's the only place we'll get a ticket to in South India. It's really off-season.'

'Yeah, listen, since we're already late, you and Sasha go score.'

Which is how I found myself heading for the railroad score. At the railroad crossing, the ghetto began. Suddenly, there were dogs and goats underfoot. The road became dirt. There was two-wheeler traffic, all laden with bales of cotton. Men sat on either side, watching as I went down the street, the only person in this area in jeans and a sweatshirt – what else could I be here for?

The bridge over the nullah was so narrow that nothing wider than a motorcycle or two pedestrians could cross it. I crossed the bridge looking down and then took the first left into the shanties. Up ahead, a little child asked me what I wanted. I gave him a five hundred. He went to the tree, and rummaged in the hanging bag. How clever – if the cops nabbed it, it wasn't in anyone's *possession*, was it?

He pulled out a five hundred package, which was the length of a loaf of bread, and threw it at me. I put it inside my sweatshirt and walked out fast. I saw a cop at the turn. He'd been paid off I hoped, and kept walking, looking down. I imagined his eyes boring into my back, and then I realized that I was wearing an NLS sweatshirt! Oh crap, oh my god. I stiffened and walked faster. Across the bridge, I ran into a side alley where a goat was being butchered. As it bleated its blood into the dirt, its fur matted brown, its eyes rolling madly, I ran past the scene, took a parallel alley and ran across the lines just ahead of the train. Safety.

At the railway station, the lines to the distant counters were too enormous for anything to be possible. The gigantic machine of the Indian Railways was clogged. Then Amlan disappeared with a faceless guy in a black leather jacket and returned with fourteen tickets in black in general class and we were tearing down the platform as the wheels began to rotate slowly, the huge clocks passing above our heads as we ran, leaping over boxes, sidestepping people, the door of the general compartment hopelessly full. Sasha took two long steps and jumped in, head first, like a bull. The last of us, Kiran, was lifted on the strength of our arms clear off the end of the platform to safety, as solid ground disappeared from beneath his feet.

Inside, all was chaos. There was a cow, women with pots, families crushed up against the walls, each seat thrice occupied. The familiar metal and plastic of Indian Railways infrastructure was obscured by a mass of warm humanity, stinking in close proximity. I spent the night suspended between the edge of an upper bunk and the opposite wall of the compartment, a chain held in the crook of an arm, like Odin, hanging between sleep and pain. When we reached Coimbatore, it was two hours before dawn. The town was awake surreally early – buses were running half full and hardware shops were open.

Around the time the sun came up over the palm trees in a muddy back lane, we were furiously eating piled up-dosas at a darshini, standing around steel tables. Then we smoked a pipe load of our weed and sipped chai till we could find the next piece of our travel puzzle.

The bus from Coimbatore stopped at Palem, where it was mid-afternoon, hot and dusty. The buses at the station looked like ephemeral beasts, shimmering unreally in the petrol fumes. The station was in the heart of the town, which itself was brown thatch, pink concrete walls, red and blue signs in Tamil. Rathore said he needed a beer. We were all coming down and it was a hot day, which made it a popular suggestion. Amlan just wanted a cold place. Our bags were weighing us down and we had three hours to our bus. Nothing is as hellish as a small Tamil town in the heat, the smell of piss rising from the gutters and the corners, the sun beating down like divine retribution. The locals stare at outsiders uncomprehendingly, as if they were animals or on television.

Suddenly, like some dude in the Bible being shown a sign by his God, we saw it around the bend, a huge blue plastic sign in English, with a wine glass in outline and the legend 'Time Pass A/C Bar and Restaurant' emblazoned on it. That is as close as I have ever come to believing in a God who answers prayers.

The bus to Kodai swung alarmingly from side to side, the rocks of the roads slipping and crunching tellingly, oncoming traffic screaming downhill fast. Amlan was wistful.

'If we die now, all the crap we've done in our lives will be forgotten.'

'Yeah, they'll put us in the papers. Tragic Accident Claims Brilliant Students in Flower of Youth.'

'Until they find the five hundreds of ganja in Rathore's bag. Then they'll fuck us posthumously.'

The spectre of our demise passed. It was bitterly cold when we reached the Kodai bus stop at eleven at night. The winding ribbon of lights led down to a small pond, from where we walked up the hill to Seshadri's house. The road became a path, the path became an alley of trees and the side of rock, all uphill, so steep at times that we had to use a handhold. We felt our way, hearing the sharp barks of big dogs seemingly always behind us. Finally, the friendly light of a fire greeted us and, behind the flames, the sight of Seshadri's groundskeeper holding back a giant Rottweiler. In minutes, we were shaking off the cold in front of a large brushwood fire on the side of a beautiful colonial-era mountain cottage. Dreams of warm beds, hot showers and soup filled my head. Then Seshadri returned with a slightly dazed look on his face.

'Guys, there's a slight problem ... I don't have the keys to the house.'

'What?'

'Did you leave them somewhere?'

'In Madras.'

We were all flabbergasted, but Rathore was a step ahead of us.

'You mean you never had them when we started up here?'

'Uh. No.'

In retrospect, what's amazing is that at this point no one lost their temper or flipped out. Clustered around the fire, under the eaves of the old colonial cottage, we rolled and smoked and talked and talked, and told stories and took the piss out of each other. Once in a while, someone would stagger off into the dark to take a leak and you'd hear a little rustling from the darkness. I remember the bone-white shine of the stars through the pines, the earth tilting on unfamiliar axes, the stars spinning around, the hard bag under my head and the difference between the freezing wind at my back and the warmth of the fire, at 9,000 feet in November in a sweatshirt.

In the light of the fire, in the chiaroscuro tableau around it, there was madness. Rathore threatened to wolfbag Raghav.

'You want to what bag him?' asked Amlan.

'Wolfbag him. You kids never heard of wolfbagging before?'

'Not till date. Pray enlighten us.'

'See, this is how I do it. Raghav, your assistance is required.'

'Go fuck yourself.'

'No. No. You want to do this.'

'Come on, da,' Sasha urged, 'be a sport.'

Raghav groaned and stood up.

Rathore, in his element like a Vegas showman, 'Not like that. Assume the Position.'

'What?'

'Shut up and bend over, dude. You're killing the moment,' hissed Amlan.

Rathore continued, 'So, let's say I'm fucking Raghav in the ass.'

'Saying, no touching,' growled Raghav.

'Quiet, bitch. So, yeah, we are gents of a certain persuasion and I am persuaded, perhaps, minded to anally pleasure my friend here,' he tapped Raghav on the ass, 'and so we begin, you know, all meat and potatoes.' He mimed a gentle rhythmic humping and Raghav protested vehemently.

'Right, sorry. Got carried away. So, if I want something a little special, here's what I do. I tie one end of a long thread around a raw strip of bacon, and make Raghav swallow it, and leave the string hanging out of his mouth. Now, cometh the hour, cometh the man ...'

Rathore put his hand forward. Raghav stiffened. '... and then just as I am, so to speak, cometh, I yank the bacon out, and he throws up, and because it's a natural reaction, his sphincter clenches, and I nail it like a fucking cowboy while it lasts.'

As we are helpless with laughter, Rathore grabbed Raghav by the shoulders and started really humping him hard and letting out wolf howls. Raghav squealed like a pig and leapt forward into the fire, kicking and cussing and spreading the flaming logs about.

In the morning, we woke stiff and grouchy and staggered off down the hill, dying for breakfast, a place to crap, coffee and somewhere to spend the next night, preferably with walls and a roof. By the time we had everything all together, it was late afternoon and the lake was clouding over. We rented bicycles to see what Kodai had to offer and, more importantly, to find mushrooms. Riding in the stoned mist, we could barely keep track of each other, confused by the lights of cars, the sounds across the water in the clear mountain air. Amlan went off to score mushrooms in the bazaar. Raghav and Rathore sat on the embankment and rolled joints of increasing complexity. Rockets, cannons, tulips – they all issued forth from their digits, an arsenal of smoke.

Meanwhile, Sasha rode ahead of me, his calves pumping the cycle up the mountain road and into the mist. I followed, suddenly aware that there was nobody behind me. We must have lost our way, because nothing familiar showed up ahead. Then, off the narrow road, a mud track covered in pine needles opened up. It went up the hillside, steep enough to force us off our bikes. We left them lying on the ground and walked on, till we came upon an old stone gate, covered in ivy, the entrance to a graveyard. It had clearly been abandoned in favour of more central locations quite some time ago and now was the province of trees and silence. In that fading hour of the evening, Sasha and I walked up the gravel path, passing the tombs of officers who served a queen on the other side of the planet. Before us rose two giant trees, with trunks as wide as cars, the path passing between them.

Now this is the strangest thing, and I don't know why you would believe me, but I swear it's the truth. Neither of us could bring ourselves to cross the invisible line between the trees; there was something deep and dark and profoundly sinister on that path, and crossing that line would put us in its realm. Centuries of stored-up death lay on guard there, waiting. Even Sasha, whom I had to pull out of fights with autodrivers, cops, teachers, who I had never seen afraid, and never would again, was at that moment truly afraid. But because he was the sort of man who defied his fears, he stepped across and came back. We returned to the path, where there was enough light for us to find our bikes. We didn't speak throughout and never spoke of it again, but that day, I felt like I had seen an entrance to the underworld, like Odysseus. Sometimes, I think that some things are meant to be left alone and maybe Sasha should never have crossed that line, but had to, because he was that sort of person.

On returning to the group near Raghav's cottage, we smoked a few joints. Then, since Amlan had managed to score mushrooms, we ate the little twirled up brown mushies on bread, sour and rubbery. The shamans and the gurus and the wild men of the mountains got it right – they really are a window into the world of God. The mind stays attached to its rational self, but the senses contort like playful dolphins in the water. When you turn to look at what you thought you saw out of the corner of your eye, it's actually still there. The line between reality and possibility is smudged till it is faint.

Just as things were starting to get a little odd, we decided now would be a good time to navigate our way to our new lodgings from Seshadri's house. Down a stone path that was shining like water in the moonlight, we walked into a forest where the trees placed logs in our path. The twigs moved at my feet and I was afraid that they might be snakes until I remembered that there are no snakes at that altitude. The forest was completely dark and no moonshine pierced through the canopy. Our two torches found each other once in a while, creating a solid out of two beams of light. I recall a glow strip on a backpack being my personal pole star. Suddenly I saw, or I thought I saw, a faun peeking out at me from behind a tree. I blinked and he was no longer there, but higher up in the tree, there were faces carved into the bark, which smiled at me. The darkness was full of faces, full of beguiling barky smiles and twinkling eyes. If we hadn't all been together, it is entirely possible I would have spent the whole night in the enchanted forest. Miracle of miracles, we found the cottage we were renting by the light of the torch. The mirrors seemed bent to me, and the candlelight revealed little halos around Seshadri and Rathore. Sasha looked like an evil elf, making a water-bong with the only pen in miles. We sat and smoked till we passed out that night and everything got redder and redder till it was bright red, and we were submerged in a maraschino cherry liquid.

Let nobody tell you pot isn't drugs. Maybe it isn't, if you smoke once a week, even if you smoke once a day. But if you smoke heroically and single-mindedly, like Snoop or the Method Man, burning through handfuls of grass daily, you will find yourself addicted. Fuck, if you eat chocolate the way the Method Man smokes pot, you would find yourself addicted to chocolate and forty kilos overweight.

Increasingly, our travels in these realms intensified. I went for chemicals in a big way; uppers, downers, pain pills, sleepers. Raghav's inclination for coke would have been a problem if it wasn't just so damn expensive. Sasha liked the occasional bit of ecstasy. With Rathore, you'd have to reword the question. Were there any drugs Rathore didn't like? No, there were not.

Drugs had become the one holy and true thing for us; the quest for the boundaries of the mind, for the other side of reality's coin, our one real adventure. We were all brave psychonauts, each willing the other to go the step further, to advance our own science of experience. Nothing mattered more to us at that point than to experience better living through chemistry, to see the hidden tigers in the tree tops, the waves in the sky, the elasticity of human faces, to live life bigger and brighter, like in a movie directed by a chess grandmaster.

The return journey was sober because we couldn't score any. In three days, we had run through about a kilo of weed. Walking into the acad block that night, my bag over my shoulder, wearing a pair of shorts and my big scuffed black hiking boots, I felt defiantly cool; like Appetite-era Axl Rose cool. I found Jennifer, sitting on the steps waiting for me, and grabbed hold of her and felt her softness embrace me. She clung to me jealously and I know that I had never been prouder than I was at that moment. Standing there with my girl, I owned the tame suburban night.

lost in the supermarket

The Clash/London Calling/1979

I'm in Hyderabad, but it's not the Hyderabad we visited with the team, our studs, shin-guards and stockings in the large kitbag we took turns carrying. It's not the fragrant oriental Hyderabad of camel haleem and old havelis and markets full of exotic forgotten arts. This is a Hyderabad I could have done with not seeing.

It's two in the morning and I'm on the outskirts of the city, in a building that's a glass-and-plastic shell. It's an infrastructure and mining company, and I'm in the data room doing diligence. I'm all alone. I have Dhruv on the phone whenever I need him, but I'm the only warm body in this building right now.

In a way, I'm glad that Sasha never had to do this – it's hard on the self-image. I've been going through piles of documents and making notes on them for the last four days. Infrastructure contracts, government approvals, joint venture agreements, share subscriptions, share purchase agreements and now finally these: loan documents.

Loan documents are what you diligence the most carefully, because they are the ticking time bombs under companies. The first time I saw one of these, I felt dizzy, because I could not imagine anybody putting their name to so draconian a document. But everybody does and, as a result, there's a shadow world of negotiations between banks and companies that lawyers never see. For example, a company may have entered into an agreement with a financial covenant like a debt service cover ratio. Now, if it defaults on the condition, the bank can declare a default and enforce the security, which will always be worth more than the loan to the company. This leads to a situation where the bank always has the company's balls in its cold clammy grasp. To avoid the squeeze, in addition to servicing the loan, the company pays safety money to the bank.

My personal favourite clause is a 'cross default'. The cross default clause states politely that if the borrower defaults on any indebtedness to any lender, the lender in this agreement may declare a default under the agreement with this bank.

Just imagine that! A company this size would have somewhere in the region of Rs 4,000 crore in indebtedness. Now, if one of those hundreds of financial covenants is violated, and the bank isn't quickly placated, it will declare a default. Then any other bank with a cross default clause in its agreement (and they all have one) is also entitled to declare a default. Basically, that entire Rs 4,000 crore that the company has borrowed becomes immediately due. So the wolf is at the door and the company's fucked because it doesn't have the cash to cover the debt. No company ever does, because everyone's been taught in management school that 3:1 is a safe debt-to-equity ratio.

If all this goes off and bankruptcy happens, somebody will file a suit for winding up as a pressure tactic. From there, it's all downhill to the Debt Recovery Tribunals and the Company Court, the liquidators and the bank's counsel in black robes all trying to get the court to cut them a good deal. Or the company gets bought out for pennies on the pound, the management get shiny parachutes and the shareholders bottom out.

All of this could happen if some finance officer at the company doesn't take care to read every line of this loan document and comply with it. If I was that guy, it would give me the greasy shits. But I'm not.

Tonight, like many nights, I worry about the people I serve. There's a phantom cloud of illusions and fictions that holds them at bay. I'm on a retainer with a law firm. That firm has entered into a mandate with this company for certain legal advice relating to an offer of shares. The shares will be offered on the open market and, if the issue is successful, the company will raise more working capital. Said like that, using the prescribed terms, it sounds all above board, distant and even slightly boring – a mechanical process.

But I look out this window tonight and I know that there are armies of earthmovers and drilling vehicles ready to move into open pit mines at dawn to extract ore from the earth. I know that they've bought a mining lease from the government, which permits them to drill into a mountain like hungry earthworms. I know that there are tribals camped out on the mountain tonight ready to link hands and spread out at dawn to prevent the big yellow machines from breaking earth on what is their Olympus, their Mount Kailash, the place where their children go to have visions and return as men.

What does this have to do with me? For two months on this deal, I've been drafting a document that the company will file with the stock exchanges and the SEBI, which will allow them to ask people for money in exchange for equity. With this money, they will buy more leases, enter into more agreements to dig into the earth and come out with dull ores, which will go into fiery furnaces and come out as the shiny hunks of metal we know, which will go to factories and become knives and forks and buildings. That's fine, but somewhere there will be a festering sore in the skin of the earth that no one will fill. There will be a magic mountain full of holes that no god will live in.

I will move on next month and work for some other company doing something else. But I can't shake the feeling that some of the dirt from that mountain will stick to my hands forever, even if I only shuffle paper all day.

You're gonna have to serve somebody, the man says. It's something you can't say in this world, but I'd like it not to be these people.

When most people think of the law, they see Gray's Inn in London, bewigged barristers, black gowns, judges with gavels. They see the high whalebone arches of grand courtrooms, monogrammed cutlery, silver-backed hairbrushes and full-length mirrors. They see students with leather-bound law reports sitting up late on green baize tables under high gothic arches. These lawyers inhabit the same world as Cicero and Locke and Mohammed Ali Jinnah. We were taught these things too – that by thinking hard, thinking big pure thoughts, we could become the secret rulers of the world. Maybe there is a way, but I doubt this is it.

I become evasive when people ask whether I do civil or criminal, or when they corner me at parties and start asking questions. I don't know these things. I do know some other things. I know the tools and ways of Mammon. I understand how funds can acquire stakes in companies. I understand how escrow agreements work. I know Rupee Facility Agreements and Debt Subordination Agreements and letters of comfort.

My world is not made of leather and silver cutlery and green baize. It's plastic and glass. My tools are my Outlook inbox and my BlackBerry. When I refer to precedent, I don't reach for a reporter. I open the folder on the network drive corresponding to the last time that clause was used and cut and paste it. They call it 'tracking'; why should anything new ever be drafted? Mammon craves consistency. As long as things go as they always have, million-dollar agreements will be executed and the rich will get richer.

The priests of Mammon are the bankers, who come from the magic lands across the oceans, from Morgan Stanley, Merrill Lynch, Lehman Brothers, from the glinting pyramids of New York and Singapore. In the crystal chambers inside those pyramids, sheaves of paper money are blown about on powerful crosswinds. All day, they jump up and down, gathering enough to line their pockets, and then they learn how to talk about the bigger picture, and driving the process and creating value.

Once upon a time, I used to find all of this very sexy. I would say as much to Sasha often and he reluctantly came to agree, and was ready to sign on the line when the time came. But I remember his original view from that day in the Lodhi Gardens when we were both interning in Delhi.

Sasha loved Delhi, the city of mad king Tughlaq and high red walls; green patches and white bungalows and its big directionless roads and traffic circles.

That afternoon, we met near the Bada Gumbad. I had come from the corporate office where I was sorting trademark applications and I was in my formals. He was waiting on the grass, in dirty white pyjamas, a yellow T-shirt and a black coat, looking like a Nepali tea vendor. He had on a prayer cap he bought at the Jama Masjid and there was crudely applied kajal at the corners of his eyes. We talked in the afternoon about these things, about the majesty of the Supreme Court, the griminess of filing counters, the bribery of cops, the machine of the law.

'Sasha, it takes ten years to start earning in court. I don't want to wait. Why should I wait? What's the point of being poor in your twenties?'

'You've got to suffer a little. It's not so bad. There are guys who'll pay fifteen a month.'

I wanted to scream with frustration. 'Dhingra Partners starts you at eighty a month! Why should I wait? And I want a nice office and a car and an AC! Why do you want to drudge for fifteen years to get to that stage?'

He was silent for a long time, his cap angled back on his head in the golden afternoon. Suddenly he asked me, 'What do you want from life? The money or the fame?'

'Both ideally, na. Besides, couldn't the money buy you fame?'

A bear ambled onto the grass. The trainer beat a tambourine and the bear rose on its hind legs, holding its paws out in the air. Its eyes had lines of yellow rime running from them down to his snout, muzzled with old leather and brass. It was a small bear. I couldn't imagine it needing a muzzle.

'That's not the kind of fame I'm talking about.'

The bear danced at the end of its leash and, when it put its forepaws down, its back slumped gratefully. When it ambled away, we went down the street for a beer and didn't ever continue that conversation.

I didn't understand then that it was a kind of test – I didn't even understand its phrasing. He didn't mean celebrity; he meant fame. Fame can't be bought. There is no exchange rate for fame. In fact, for that flavour of fame, you must pick your course of action very wisely, and you must steer the fuck clear of celebrity.

He was hungering for something invisible to me. The fame he wanted has words that label it better, but cannot describe it. He meant greatness, greatness like Alexander of Macedonia, the greatness of kings. Greatness has a content, it is not subjective. Being great at something doesn't make you great – you must matter to humanity. You must draw the gaze of the stars.

He always asked me if I really loved the idea of what I was heading into, and I said yes, of course I did. Maybe I had just loved the high thin scent of money and that filtered everything. Insider trading, private equity, hedge funds, schemes of arrangement, asset purchases, creeping acquisitions, convertible instruments, debt stripping; let them all roll over your tongue. Say them slowly and out loud; sibilant and larcenous, they all sound like money. The context of suits and expensive ties and BlackBerries beeping was just the petri dish for these dreams of money to take hold, to dig their way in.

When damming the Narmada was a big deal, Sasha and I used to talk about Arundhati Roy, sitting on my red blanket, arguing. He used to call her a publicity hound and an enemy of progress, partly because he loved the Nehruvian project of Statehood – the big steel machine working for everyone. I used to point out that the water would go to golf courses and jacuzzis, and that the plan benefited all the worst people, while uprooting the ones the State had the greatest duty to serve. I suppose I used to say that kind of thing because I felt like a Benthamite, with a suspicious mind tending towards conspiracies.

By the end, we had flipped polarities. I had fallen in love with this world of loan documents and producing money out of thin air, of powering shiny financial machines, and Sasha spent more time wearing khadi and smoking beedis with the sort of people the State was supposed to be protecting.

Maybe if we had joined work in the same month, like we had planned, if we had kept counsel with each other, we'd have flipped polarities again, or have come to some consensus. But I don't like to think of Sasha diligencing loan documents at night. The same way he wouldn't like me eating this shit biryani the office guy has left for me. Maybe more of Hyderabad's biryani is shit than I thought. Or maybe it's who you eat it with.

That day, after Osmania University had ripped us a new one (5-1, our goal being a penalty Raghav had dived to earn), Sasha, Kelkar and I wandered through the congested market looking for a place where Kelkar could get his knee stitched up. He had gone in for a completely unnecessary tackle on a rock-covered pitch and there was a three-inch-long gash in the side of his knee. In a hole in the wall, a grinning bearded old man cleaned the wound out with spirit and grinned even more when Kelkar yelped. Then he stitched it up neatly with a length of black catgut; ten small crosses to mark the extent of his stupidity. We walked down the street and we had biryani as white as snow, with the juicy chunks of a blameless lamb falling apart under our fingers. I could eat biryani anywhere in Hyderabad tonight and it would turn to ashes in my mouth.

everything in its right place

Radiohead/Kid A/2000

The Patiala House Courts in July. Heat marries Humidity. They have two children – Sweat and Madness. Sweat takes up residence in every crevice of your body, on every surface, suspended between every two hairs. Your body is emptying itself out gradually. Madness sneaks into your head and seduces your brain. Madness whispers to it, caresses it, mounts it. No wonder no Indian philosopher ever advocated a militant theory of free will; in this weather, it's a laughable fiction. It would take a Genghis Khan to feel free in this climate.

The broad trees stretch out over the former residence of the Maharaja of Patiala and, equally, over the ignoble hovels clustered about it. Out of the hovels and the lone fruit shack crawl hundreds of lawyers in their black-and-whites, their faces glistening with sweat, their hands heavy and beringed on their cell phones. They talk loudly and move with great purpose and brusqueness. Walking amongst them are policemen holding under-trials by the hand. When you look closely, you realize that the policemen are gripping their fingers sideways, so they can break those fingers with a quick twist. The law, you see, has decreed handcuffing to be inhumane and a last resort – hence, this elegant Third World solution, the finger-lock.

This is manifestly not my practice area. I'm here, in a band and black coat, natch, because a matter needs watching and I am to observe and report to the client what happened here. It's a bail matter and the detenu is management in a company our client is interested in acquiring. So I hang back and watch the detenu's lawyer pray for bail. He raises all the arguments I remember learning, and its thrillingly simple and similar to what I remember. He pleads that no prima facie case is made out, that the evidence has been collected, that his client has deep roots in society and is unlikely to abscond, that no possible prejudice would be caused. His lawyer has the bearing of a courtroom brawler who has grown thick and calm with experience. He's out, I'm sure. There he goes. When he offers to submit to any bond the judge might set, it is offhand and casual and already done.

But it's never this simple. The public prosecutor stands up and says the magic words. He is thin and his coat is dirty. And he hits hard. 'Lordship, investigation is not over yet. CBI is filing an additional chargesheet and the ED is possessed of the matter.'

Oh, the Enforcement Directorate and the Central Bureau of Investigation, our very own KGB and Star Chamber, the bright unyielding light of justice focused through the high-powered lens of the indignation of the nation, shining straight into the eyes of the guilty. If such persons are yet to bear, what poor additional chief metropolitan magistrate is going to let an old man out of jail? What price then his elevation to the High Court?

Bail denied; petition dismissed. I can turn and leave and go back to 22° Celsius and civilization. It's a pity though, I'm thinking. The summer is terrible but, in winter, this could be fun. As I stand to leave, I stop to let in an influx of people; a girl in a white salwar kameez, chubby and cute, probably here with her parents.

It's just about lunchtime at the office, I think. I can watch this for a while. It's a main matter, so the crush is over. I take a seat.

She takes the stand. The judge directs the courtmaster to administer the oath to her. She takes it quietly. Her cross-examination begins. Her lawyer is sitting, relaxed, in a chair, waiting. Her parents are in chairs towards the back of the room. The cross-examining counsel stands and clears his throat.

'What is your age, Shweta?'

'Nineteen.'

'What studies are you doing?'

'B.A. Honours, English, in Bhagalpur College, Karol Bagh.'

'Where do you live? Do you live with your parents?'

'Yes, I stay with the parents, in Lodi Colony Government Quarters.'

'How do you travel to college? Karol Bagh to Lodi Colony is some distance, is it not?'

'I take the bus in the morning. In the evening, I take the bus back or I take the auto back, if I'm getting late.'

'I do not understand. When do your classes end?'

'They end at 2.30 p.m.'

'But buses are running in the afternoon. Why would you have to take an auto back?'

'Sometimes I get late. I have some after-college activities, musical activities.'

'On days when you have your musical activities, what time do they end? Do you always go straight back home after they end?'

'My music classes end at 6.30 p.m. Sometimes, if I'm meeting friends in the evening, I get late. Then I take an auto.'

'So you do some musical activity for four hours, and then you meet friends and come back home late at night in autos. How safe do you feel at night?'

'Normally, I am home by 9 p.m. If I'm getting very late, somebody drops me home.'

'Somebody drops you home? Earlier you had said you take autos if you are getting late. I remind you, Shweta, that you are under an oath to tell the truth. Who drops you home after 9 p.m., Shweta? Do you have a boyfriend?'

'I have a boyfriend. Sometimes he drops me home.'

'How long has he been your boyfriend?'

'About four months.'

'Is he your first boyfriend? Remember, Shweta, your oath to tell the truth ...'

'He is not my first boyfriend.'

'How many boyfriends have you had before this boyfriend?'

A pause. She looks at her parents. 'Maybe three boyfriends.'

The examining counsel smells blood in the water. 'Maybe? Why are you unsure? Did you ever have many boyfriends at the same time? Why do you not know an exact number of boyfriends?'

'Three boyfriends before.'

'So you have had four boyfriends? How young were you when you had your first boyfriend?'

'Fifteen.'

'You've had boyfriends since you were fifteen years old? Now, answer truthfully, are you a virgin?'

'Yes, I am a virgin.'

'Remember your oath, Shweta. You have filed an FIR saying you were raped. I put it to you that, if you are a virgin, your FIR was a false information and, therefore, you are subject to prosecution.'

'No, sorry, I am not a virgin.'

'But we know that. How can you have been a virgin in the first place with "maybe" four boyfriends? Shweta, be truthful, we have your medical report on record, when did you lose your virginity?'

She doesn't know where to look. She looks at me. 'Seventeen.'

'So, you have been sexually active for two years? You must be used to it by now. Do you find it painful or do you enjoy it?'

'I enjoy it.'

'And how many times have you had sex?'

'I don't know. Maybe twenty times?'

'You don't even know? At least, this you should remember, how many men have you had sex with?'

'Two.'

'Are you including the accuseds in that statement? Have you forgotten the FIR and your oath?'

'Including the accused, six.'

'Either this prosecution is unimportant to you, or what you do with your body has stopped making a difference. Now, if I may ask, do you remember the night of December 28, 2008?'

'Yes. That is the night I was raped.'

'So you say. Did you know the accused persons?'

'Yes, I knew one of them, Arpan. He was in my Modern Literature class.'

'You have stated that the accused number 1, Arpan, took you on his motorcycle. Was this voluntary?'

'Yes. He was in my class and we had talked a few times. He said he would give me a ride home.'

'Shweta, earlier in this very cross-examination, you said your boyfriend used to drop you home. Was the accused number 1 your boyfriend?'

'No! Of course not!'

'Would it be true then that you took a ride on a motorcycle from a boy who you did not know very well?'

'He was in my class. We had spoken before and I thought he was a nice boy.'

'What time did you get on this motorcycle, voluntarily?'

'It was about 10.30 p.m.'

'So, would it be correct to state that, at 10.30 p.m., you voluntarily got onto the motorcycle of a boy who was not your boyfriend?'

'Yes.'

'Then what happened?'

'He said some friends of his were drinking and I could join them.'

'Who were these friends? Can you identify them?'

'Yes. They were accused number 2, 3 and 4.'

'Had you ever met any of the accused 2, 3 or 4 prior to that night?'

'No. I had never seen them.'

'Would it be correct to say that you consumed alcoholic beverages with the accused persons?'

'Yes. There was one bottle of vodka.'

'Why did you not report this in your FIR? Since it only came out in your medical report, why should we believe anything in your FIR?'

'I couldn't say all these things in front of my parents, who went with me to file the FIR.'

'Of course, they were fine with your fornication, but not your drinking? Regardless, were you drinking on the street with the accuseds?'

'No. We had gone into one of the office buildings at Jhandewalan.'

'Was there anybody in the building?'

'I didn't see anybody. It was late.'

'Would it be correct to say that you voluntarily went into an empty building with four young men to drink liquor and spend time?'

'I thought we were only going to drink. I didn't think they would hurt me.'

'The police recovered condoms from the site. When you have sex with your boyfriends, do you use condoms?'

'Yes, of course.'

'On the night of December 28, 2008, assuming this act happened as per the FIR, which is severely doubtful given your contradictions, were condoms used?'

'Yes. They used condoms, but it wasn't because I wanted condoms to be used! I didn't want to have sex with anyone!'

'So you say. I put it to you that you had voluntarily travelled late at night on a motorcycle, voluntarily entered an empty building, voluntarily consumed alcohol with the accuseds, voluntarily had sexual intercourse with the accuseds. Is this true?'

'NO! Of course not! I'm not mad.'

'Nobody said you were mad. But I put it to you that you are wanton, habituated to sex from an early age and frequently indulging in drinking alcohol. Do you deny this?'

'Of course!'

Suddenly I feel there is not enough air in the room, that my tongue is choking my throat. I hate the counsel examining the girl. I hate the public prosecutor for not kicking up a fuss, for having seen this too many times to lose his cool. I hate the judge for not protecting her. I hate the typist for taking all of this down quietly and faithfully, for this evil to endure. I hate the mistake that led Shweta into that stairwell.

I stumble out of the courtroom, and walk into the sunshine, through the early lunch lawyers eating sweet potato chaat under the trees, in the shadow of all this crime. I get into the first auto I see and take it back to the office, undoing my band in a hurry, crumpling the stiff white strip up and tossing it out of the auto. Contempt of court, you say? Why, yes, I do have contempt for the court.

Back at my desk, I look around. It's cold and quiet. I have space for my work and my possessions. My seat is soft and padded, my screen is dusted. There is a bottle of cold water and a clean glass. My phone connection, my reference materials, my postcards on the softboard, my deals outlined in an Excel printout, my future shining clear like a diamond. Forget the dirt and scum. You've worked hard and played the game right, boy. You don't have to do that shit for a living. No murderers, rapists and thieves, only bankers and businessmen, front-page deals and fancy hotels, silk ties and nice wines, vacations and investments. The darkness is without. Forget it.

savoy truffle

The Beatles/White Album/1968

To really explain the whole thing from the absolute beginning, we need to go back to the first week of the last trimester of third year, when we were sitting in Drafting of Pleadings, being screeched at interminably by Ramnatha, the crazy old coot, with his psychotic love of exactitude, his procedural rectitude, his sadistic sense of humour. I suppose I could go down to Bangalore and meet him. He's still there, teaching procedure, Rhadamanthus with a chalkboard.

How many days we spent in the back of the class, watching time slide by glacially. There was always one person passed out in the front row, the numbers increased by approximately one per row till, at the very end of the class, everyone was asleep. Interspersed with the sleeping were the newspaper readers, students of literature, the notebook conversationalists and the habitual messagers. On the wings of the class, Amlan and Kelkar would have slipped out of their chairs and be asleep on the floor near the wall, using their bags as pillows.

All of this was perfectly acceptable because Ramnatha Reddy was oblivious to the class. In fact, he was oblivious to the twenty-first century. It was a narrow call as to whether he was in the ken about the twentieth. If you don't know him, maybe I should begin by telling you how old Ramnatha is.

Ramnatha is as old as time. He was young in the beginning of the world. When the seas cooled and the continents stopped shaking, Ramnatha walked around curiously, wide-eyed at the scale of change. He spent the Cretaceous and the Jurassic finding his way through ferns and giant club-like palms. The first creatures to leave the sea were much like shellfish and Ramnatha was pleased to enjoy them with a little sea salt and a side of thick fruit. In the times of the dinosaurs, he swam with the ichthyosaurs and ate eggs from the nests of the pterodactyl. They were most tangy and pleasant. When the large meat-eating dinosaurs approached his lean-to, he told them firmly to go away, and that they were acting beyond their rightful jurisdiction, and that they must cease from causing any damage forthwith. When the time of the dinosaurs came to an end, Ramnatha sniffed at the sudden warm weather and prepared for the coming ice ages with judicious use of woollens.

When the cities of Nineveh and Babylon were built, and the dimensions of roads and houses were settled, Ramnatha informed everyone involved that no one should build so as to block another's window or door, for those were easementary rights. When Hammurabbi laid down his famous code, it was not without Ramnatha's expertise and exactitude that the provisions regarding enforcement and procedure were laid down. Which is why Hammurabbi's laws were better and clearer than Mosaic law. Imagine, if you will, Ramnatha screeching: 'An eye for an eye? Who will see to the removal of eyes and their storage? Is there no provision for the appointment of a receiver of eyes?'

At the time of the crusades, Ramnatha saw the Levant bathed with blood and said, 'Oh no, not again.' When Columbus started mucking around in the Caribbean, he thought, 'No good will come of this.' He bet against the fall of Constantinople and the use of gunpowder; it seemed fairly counterintuitive. As an old, old man, he was shocked by the French Revolution and a little taken aback by some of the fancy newfangled ideas that were awash in Europe.

When the British sailed into Madras, Ramnatha was on the shore, watching with a frown. However, he was overjoyed with the establishment of the Presidency and mofussil courts, deeming them a vast improvement over arbitrary justice. He roundly chastised the young whippersnappers who were naming political parties after what he thought was a sexual act, telling young Bal Gangadhar Tilak to shut his mouth until his elders and betters had spoken. He thought the Government of India Act of 1935 was the last really important law to be passed.

It's quite disappointing then to think of him as a mere child of the 1920s. Even though he was already practising law when the Constitution came into existence, was vastly excited by the introduction of cinema to India and was already senile before I was born – the '20s don't seem long enough ago for the way Ramnatha looked.

I guess I'm going to have to admit to this one; it all started with something I said. I was done with the newspaper already, with the book I had brought to class and I had sent messages to all the people I could. Jenni and I were fighting about something. She was on the other side of the classroom, rigid and imperious. Let her stew, I thought.

'Kiran, da. I have an idea.'

'Hmmm?'

'Let's barbeque on the terrace'

'Are you serious? Zoju, you choot, it's really complicated.'

'It's quite simple. I'll look up some recipes.'

'And do what! We don't even have a barbeque.'

'We just need a cheap grill. Shouldn't cost more than some thousand bucks. Come on! We'll figure it out – we're men, it'll come naturally to us, right?'

At that point, Kiran should really have seen a giant neon sign above my head that read 'This Way Lies Trouble'. Instead, he saw opportunity.

Kiran was like that, back then. He would take ideas as they came and, if they contained one plausible germ in them, would run himself into the ground to make them happen. Sometimes I think he enjoyed organizing things more than participating in them. The grill was actually cut to order for us by a steel worker up the street. In my head, I can see Kiran in the sun holding his hands apart and frowning decisively, explaining what he was looking for. The grill was delivered to Kiran's room and we went over to marvel at the neat little creature as she lay there, Kiran lying on his bed with affected languor and not a little pride.

Four days later, we decided to get to it. Money was collected and a list of desiderata made. Kiran and I took Raghav's car to Johnson Market, to buy phal slices from the butcher there. It poured all the way and the wipers had conked out. We sat in the car, in the interminable traffic of

Mysore Road, under the long trees, and listened to old dance music, with the bass up way too high. The outside world disappeared into a running haze.

'She's not really hot that way, just, you know, attractive, easy to talk to.'

'Don't lie, it's not like you actually talk to girls.'

'Dude, it's about all I get to do.'

'It's alright. As Amlan says, all the trouble in the world comes from trying to dip your dong where the odds are long.'

In Johnson Market, the early hungry were already there, thronging around Siddiqui, where getting food is some part a test of your flexibility and some part your wrestling skill. Up the street were the butchers, a long corridor lit by bulbs hanging from wires off the arched ceiling. On hooks, like brutal works of art, were haunches, were legs, were shoulders, and then inedible things I could not name. The butcher was an old god of slaughter, sitting in his bloodied haven, slapping flesh on his slab and on the scales. It was still raining outside, but drippily, more like a loose faucet than the downpour we had on the way in. We could barely lift the bag when we left.

We went then to the tiny meat shops up the street in Chandra Layout, where sweaty Portuguese men blowtorch chickens to tighten them up and dry up the blood. The shop itself was dark and smelly, where concrete and blood-hardened wood lived uncomfortably with the colourful calendars on the wall.

Down the street, we bought a large orange plastic tub, a knife and tongs. We bought butter too, in cakes, curd, chilli and fresh mint. It was dark in Nagarbhavi, as we cruised down the street, buying potatoes, onions, soy sauce and another tub. Our room had taken on the semblance of a storehouse crossed with a butcher's.

I had seen it done before, but when the implicit trust of a dozen people lies on your shoulders and all you are equipped with is a large bag of packets and an absurd orange tub, things are different. I sat down in my room and chucked the lot of them into the tub, with an insouciance I did not feel. We ordered more curd, calling Amlan frantically and ordering other forgotten domestic ingredients. While I was sitting on my floor in my shorts, creating the yellow-white marinade for the chicken, Kelkar stood at a table with two bags of meat, shirtlessly cutting slits in the chicken. Nothing will bring out the butcher instinct in a man like eight kilos of raw meat and a sharp knife. I then ran the eight kilos of thin beef slices into a bigger tub and carefully massaged them into a single soaking brownish substance, with the mint leaves clumping on it.

On the roof there was a breeze and the night was clear and starry and, where we sat, the trees of Bangalore University and the outlying land waved symphonically. Amlan lit the fire after only a few minutes of cursing.

The first batch went on and there was a delicious sizzle when the hot black metal first encountered flesh. Sitting there, tongs in hand, lemons ready, shirts off, we were the kings of the world, who had cracked it and done what no one else had in memory. We were raucous, we were proud and the meat, when it came off the fire, bore up to it. It was a swooning kind of tender and, when you bit down, there was the satisfying crunch of chunky pepper and buttery smoothness. Each of us took turns being grillmaster that night, took calls as to whether the batch on the grill was done, whether it should be turned over.

We liked to fan the flames as high as they would go. We would open up the side door, roll up sleeves, pick up the plate and set to. The faces we made: we would grimace, suck in air in huge lungfuls and speak in a breathless clipped way. Strictly speaking, it was unnecessary except when the fire was being lit. In fact, the best meat comes off the slow fire. It's softer, better done inside and tastes smokier. But we enjoyed fanning and everyone enjoyed watching the fanning, the flames licking the grill grease and spitting. So we kept fanning. Inter Milan were playing Man United in the Champions League match on at the time and the score floated up to us occasionally.

With the exception of Seshadri, we didn't achieve as much as a lot of people we went to college with. We could all have landed jobs with international law firms, United Nations agencies; we could have wangled scholarships to Ivy League colleges; we could have edited books and published papers. We didn't work for it. When something happened to make us proud, we cherished it. In Law School, no one will compliment you unless they have to or they're getting something out of it. To survive, you learnt pride and self-confidence. That night we felt both things.

There are pictures of that night, of the delirious joy and brotherhood we felt, of the simple male pleasure of cooking meat for ourselves, an idea carried flawlessly from conception to fruition at the cost of a hundred bucks a head. There's a picture of Amlan, black and sardonic smile lit up by a cigarette, inspecting the grill. There's one of all of us sweating together blissfully. There are pictures of creamy marinated meat, roasted dark meat and the endless flickering flames of the coals. There's one of Sasha grinning like a moron, a makeshift water-bong of his own manufacture in his hand.

Seshadri ate what would come to be the most troublesome potato of his life that night, though he didn't know it then. We were extraordinarily careful about it. It did not come near the meat knife. It rested in fresh coals, under a meat-free area of the grill-top. He was that sort of strict vegetarian.

It was only at five, after so many rounds that the chicken was done and only a few kilos of the beef were left, that we disbanded, staggering off the terrace, unable to eat any more. The beef was slipped into a bag, and like everything else, left up top to be dealt with the next day.

We should just have chucked it, like a booze bottle, into ISEC and let nature take care of the carrion. These things were planned, but they were never executed, because we were just that lazy. The grill was cleaned off fondly, the plates washed and everything returned to Kiran's room.

There was one thing we forgot to take care of. The bag – the leftover meat and the bones and fat. It sat there when people smoked at night. It sat there when people went up to ponder during the day. It was there in the afternoon after class, dull in the sunshine. It sat there like a bad omen.

I wonder often why we did nothing about it. We're not stupid people. It's just that it was part of the way we lived our lives, hoping for unpleasant tasks to be removed to the future, postponed, extended. There were many of us and somebody else would do it. No one did.

Then one day, the janitor wanted to know why the water was smelling bad and checked the tank. In the tank was a small red bag, opened, and fat and bones, floating and sinking variously.

It could not have just fallen in. It had been lifted, by someone who carried it up a twelve-foot-high platform and threw it into a tank six feet above the platform. There was a steel cover on the tank. For the longest time, everyone thought it was Sasha. After he died, no one said that anymore; maybe they still thought it. No one knows the truth of it yet, and the chances are that no one ever will. There were some truly sick fuckers in Law School at the time – the guy who wore leather boots and boxers to the loo, the lizard crucifier, the coprophiliac. Anyone could have done it, but because we were the ones there that night, it was our ass on the line.

There were show-cause notices up on the boards before lunch that day. Our reputations had suddenly gone to zip. Suddenly, we were defilers of religious sentiment, polluters of water resources, the degraded immoral detritus of society and guilty under fifteen sections of the Indian Penal Code. Naturally, people helpfully testified against our characters, and everything we had ever done wrong came up. Rustication loomed large; this was an unprecedented crime and, if they could pin it on anyone, he'd get chucked out immediately.

Those notices had brought pressure from the administration on the Disciplinary Committee to catch someone, fine someone, or refer someone to them. When a matter leaves the hostel and goes to the Warden, the Director, or the Exam Department, the nature of the inquiry changes. A vicious kind of justice operates, where only those who are innocent to an improbable extent get away unscathed. There is the waiting, and the vulture-like consultations amongst faculty members, and the advice of the 'better' students is sought. It's justice by committee.

That night at the show-cause, four of us were grilled at a time by the Disciplinary Committee and the rest of us, twenty-two in all, were left out to marinate. They couldn't pin anything on us; there was too much conflicting testimony and nobody gave any names away. Ultimately, nothing came of it except a slap on the wrist, but it was clear that if we hadn't felt the love of the faculty and institution yet, it wasn't going to start now. In addition to Raghav being a rapist and us being his friends, we were all now also polluters of public morality.

Meanwhile, even before the show-causes were held, a notice had appeared banning cooking on the terraces. In two weeks, grilling in Law School had sprung into being and come to an end.

the chemicals between us

Bush/The Science of Things/1999

You can sense a break-up coming like you can smell winter on the wind. Suddenly, it becomes only a matter of time. The sense of decay works itself into every thought. There's the extra consideration when you're making plans, when you're booking tickets – *how long will this go on?*

Jennifer and I broke up on a summer afternoon at the end of third year. The sort of afternoon where the sun has been shining so long that every surface radiates heat. The silence built up like sand falling grain by grain through an hourglass.

'You love me,' she said, 'but you don't love me enough to be with me.'

I said nothing; there wasn't enough to scrape together for speech. Her face was flat as a wall, her eyes expressionless leaning towards contempt. But her fingers clenched and unclenched, crumpling the grass around her. The silence had built up into a little pile that came up to my knees.

'I don't understand. What went wrong? You got bored, didn't you?'

Silence. Silence. I looked away. Silence.

'Don't expect me to wait for you. I like having someone in my life. I love you, Zorawar, but you're not so special that no one else will ever mean anything to me.'

The gauntlet. I left it on the floor. The clock of my silence was still running.

If I had said anything then, I would have saved what we had. Why did I not? Why did I walk out on Jennifer then? Was it because I didn't enjoy her company? No. Was it because she didn't get me, or we didn't have enough in common? Far from it.

I walked because I wanted to feel novelty again. My eyes turned for a dozen women a day. I longed to see them all naked, to feel their lips on my neck, to feel their nipples hard against my chest. To feel the feeling I had felt with her when we first made love. I felt like a clock was ticking somewhere and I needed to do more people in the time I had.

One night, not two weeks after we had broken up, I was at a quad party. The sweat had soaked through my shirt and I could feel it cling to the skin on my back. Here I was doing what I had wanted to all along, hunting pussy. There's an art to scouting the dance floor for prey. Never hunt girls dancing with guys. Never hunt girls in circles of girls – a red light hangs above them. Hunt girls who hang around and don't look like they belong; or are in groups of mixed friends; or may have dressed up a bit. Hunt girls whose eyes are searching, as yours are.

And sometimes you are the prey.

I felt her approach me from behind. Turning, I was lost in the hair, her palm against my belly. Feeling her hip brush my crotch. What happens then is a Discovery documentary. The male animal is aroused but watchful; he scents the air for trouble. She brushes my crotch again with her hip, turning so that she has her back to me. It's Malaika and, as I lean in, I can smell the agriculture of rum on her breath. My hips swivel forward, the bulge of my pants meeting the valley where her buttocks meet under her skirt. Her hand reaches to hold mine and all my caution evaporates. There is no tease here, no trap. We grind and then I lead her away, to the water cooler. It is dark and I lean against it, my arm trapping her in the space between the wall and the cold cooler. I lean in and she meets me, her tongue hungrily probing my mouth and her hand slipping into the ass of my pants. The dam of restraint collapses. No law on earth, no code of propriety, no relationship could contain this pair of animals in their pants.

We stumble upstairs, away from the music, through the bars of the staircase, over to the locked part of the building beyond the classrooms. The music and laughter is a dimension away now. I sit and her breasts smother my face. With urgency, I pull her top off, her nipples glorious and upright. I lick them, turning and feeling their wetness against my cheek. She's panting, her hand urgently unzipping me, grabbing my length and pumping it. She hikes up her skirt and I rip apart her underwear, feeling the wet fabric tear under my fingers. She gasps in shock and holds me as I search my wallet for a condom, feeling the blood pounding through the rod between her fingers. Then wordlessly, I slip my cock into her and she rides me on the dark dusty steps. She rides me like a horse, rising up in her saddle and plunging back down, biting me so she wouldn't moan, trying to prevent the sound from carrying downstairs, her fingernails raking my back up and down. The smell of sex fills up the stairwell like hot air fills a balloon, and I am worried that people far below can smell it. It wouldn't have mattered even if we were setting off flares, neither of us could have stopped.

When we're finished, our fingers sticky and our breath ragged, the leaky sac of juices at our feet, we have no words between us to break the silence. Politely, we slip down the stairs and disappear in opposite directions.

With just that choice of location, I betrayed Jennifer. If you make love enough times in a bed or on a staircase, maybe it becomes holy, maybe it absorbs love. I fucked her where we used to make love, in the exact way that we used to make love. Would it have been different if I took her to the roof, or behind the tennis courts, or if we did it missionary or doggy style?

I woke up the next morning and stretched before the mirror in the bathroom. My neck was bruised with purple reminders of teeth and my chest and back red with scratches, my body a battlefield. I was so taken with those wounds, bruises and lacerations, so very turned on. It seemed that was all I wanted.

To exonerate myself, I'd like to point to a larger cultural trend here and say, no, I wasn't the only asshole. Sexual expression in India may have been thousands of years old, as old as the Kamasutra and the temples of Khajuraho, but free sex in India began in the nineties – with Madhu Sapre, Milind Soman, two pairs of white sneakers and a python. It began with Kamal Sidhu posing on a beach for KS condoms. We were the first generation of truly free sex in India. Sex via Orkut, Facebook, SMS sex, backseat sex, club sex – the first generation for whom sex was assumed. It was all around us. How could I resist? I yearned to enter this brave new latex nation of free sex, whose denizens paid each other booty calls and under whose shirts were the scratches of the previous night's wildcat.

For what I wanted, there was no better guide than Raghav. I followed him and I got what I wanted; a head full of uncertain memories of strangers and strange places. The flashing commerce of dance floors and club bathrooms; doing lines of coke off a toilet seat; the backseats of cars; the friends circles that last exactly one night; names on my phone I can't connect to faces; faces bending over me in the dark; the fumbling of uncertain hands, unknown bodies; the quick escape from a family house in the morning; the back window and drainpipe escape route. An eternity of calm proud mornings in unknown parts of town, smoking a cigarette and yawning while trying to flag down an auto, the buzz subsiding uncertainly like a man coming down a ladder. Maybe if I see her in Pecos next week or next month, I'll wave. No harm, no foul.

In that time, that misshapen year of our lives, I would go out too much. Occasionally, I would find myself bored and tired, studying my glass, thinking quiet thoughts to myself when I should have been jovial. In a sense, I felt a duty to be drunk and to be stoned, and to try my luck with every girl I saw, because I was satisfying an undertaking. I was pushing a shape into eternity, burning away a sort of mortality. There he is, I could say, embossed on the scene: Zorawar Chauhan, Bangalore, 2005, leaning against a wall, smoke curling around his hand, lean and wolfish, looking like they built the room around him. He's wearing straight jeans and chucks on his feet. The faded shirt falls off him to emphasize his leanness, his clavicles, his jaw, his earring shining under his unruly hair. Damn, he's looking good.

One winter night, I was in bed reading and I got a call from Jennifer. She had started seeing Kiran. It made all the sense in the world, a neat two-dimensional plastic puzzle where large blocks fell into place perfectly. I had pulled the string out and the picture had adjusted itself accordingly.

We had resolved to hang out and be friends – against the better counsel of Raghav. We did hang out, her, Kiran and I, as well as Amlan and Kelkar and the friends we had in common. Kiran had his brother's car, I'd borrow Sasha's or Raghav's, and we cruised to town. Finances allowing, we used to sit at Pecos till it started shutting around 11.30 p.m. and then drive back home. It would occur to me sometimes that I still hadn't filled in the gaps in my life. When I'd say goodbye, she'd hold on a little too long and her eyes would be a little sad when she'd leave. I would wonder what Kiran was thinking, but we were all so much closer to each other than would permit us to behave as boys and girls normally do.

One evening, I dropped Kiran and Amlan off and she stayed in the front seat and cried. 'It hurts,' she said, 'to not have you.' I said nothing and watched. The trees were coming together; the leaves disappearing into large dark shapes. I felt impatient to get on with my life. I had tied up the loose ends – how dare they come undone?

I looked down at the gearshift. Something shone in the half-light.

'How did this happen?' I asked holding her wrist. On it were half a dozen parallel scars. They gleamed with malevolence.

'A light bulb broke. I was cleaning it up.'

I knew that wasn't the truth. But I was no longer responsible, was I? This was no longer my cross to carry.

What I do know is that for those months that Jennifer was with Kiran, his life was beautiful. She was the queen in his chess set, the prize he got for being a great guy, for visiting his uncle and aunt every weekend, for never pushing the boundaries of excess, for being immune to the bitchiness and elbowing ambition of the world around him. When she sat on the back of his bike, his joy was beyond measure, the joy of possession of a jewel. Even emotionally damaged, Jennifer was the best thing that had happened to him in years.

Now Kiran works at TSMS Bombay. All day and most of the night, he parses through loan agreements and project finance documents, rearranging security arrangements and repackaging debt into bonds. His only pleasures are the sea he lives by and the phone calls to the new girlfriend in Delhi. He has a paunch and his limbs are weak from disuse. His laughter has an increasingly desperate edge to it. I saw him for an evening on Bandra bandstand when I went down this last time.

Out on the bandstand, our shadows are much bigger than we are. The yellow light of the apartment buildings behind us and the headlights of the occasional car, the occasional cop, turn the pavement of the promenade into a maze of gently waving fronds and stems. Kiran is smoking a Milds, one leg folded up for support against the wall. I don't want to turn around and look at anyone. In the distance, the dark sky and the dark water are one entity, out of which roiling ribbons of white appear and break on the serrated teeth of the rocks below.

I shake my head. 'You don't know how good you have it here.'

Kiran asks meditatively, 'What makes you think I don't? I took the Bombay office only to be near the sea. It'll probably be the only thing I'll miss if I leave.'

'What are you saying? You won't miss watching little Miss Bhatnagar bend over the printer?' Amlan laughs.

'Who's this Bhatnagar girl?' I ask.

Amlan points at Kiran, 'Bhatnagar's this tight little thing. Works in the tax team. Talks a lot. Kiran was hitting on her. Very one-sided flirting.'

Kiran was uncharacteristically quiet about her. 'I'm not really her type, even if I was single. Also, she talks so much shit.'

Amlan snorts at the euphemism. 'He means his bonus isn't the type of bonus she's attracted to. Kiran thought he was getting somewhere and then her partner took her to Goa for a weekend. Nice quiet weekend. The way I hear it, every time she opened her mouth, he filled it. Solved that problem.'

We're all silent for a bit. The air is thick with the unnamed ghosts of our world – money, desire, hierarchy, compliance.

Amlan is pointing up. 'I want to live in the penthouse, over there. You guys can move in below me, and the Delhi guys can take up lower floors. Anyway, prices will not be so high in the future, global warming and all.'

'We'll do our reunion with the first guy to get married from our batch.'

I can just imagine it. It'll be great. We'll all disappear into the desert for a week with ten crates of liquor and come out without any memories, minus a few camels, plus a couple of pregnancies and sick as dogs. In fact, it'll be so great that it will never actually happen. We finish smoking and head off. I go to my hotel to finish work. They go home to the flat they share.

The distance has changed everyone. The community we shared once is now a little uncertain. You have to call ahead and plan and scheme and take days off to meet people. You have to squirrel away to hotel rooms at night and drink from the mini-bar because everything else in any town is shut by the time you get off work.

I'd like to think things are okay between Kiran and myself now, but I can't. We slip from comfort and laughter into uncertainty and emptiness so easily. Of course, once it wasn't even cordial. At the time, we had the mien of gentleman duelling, an unstated sporting affair for the soul of Jennifer.

nightswimming

R.E.M./Automatic for the People/1992

Maybe because it's a late night and I am looking out of the window above the coffee machine at the empty street outside, a night long gone resurfaces. The parking lot is empty, except for my car. The coffee machine whirrs and grinds out its melancholy lament. There's a familiar yearning filling me, a hunger for the carousel world of liquor and travel and sex.

It is almost midnight before Raghav and I get back from Surya. There's a slight buzz around us, but we're far from drunk. The grass is fresh and green and the trees wave gently in and out of the golden pools of light. The breeze is invigorating and we're too wide awake to call it a night. The prospect of pot on the terrace does not excite us. As we come to the main gate, Sasha's white 800 is parked at the side. The line is extended and the catch reeled in. I reach into my pocket and dial him, realizing how futile the action is. His phone is probably lying under his bed, or in his bucket – anywhere but his pocket, and there's no chance that he's in his room.

But serendipity is riding shotgun again. Sasha hoves into view in a pair of white shorts and a kurti. Raghav has checked out the Acad block to rustle up more trouble, and returns with it in tow in the form of Malaika. Sasha was last seen with her in the car two nights ago, and I am magnanimous enough to grant that this is his streak and should continue.

We get into the car and pull out just as the gates are closing behind us for the night. I'm driving, Raghav's in the passenger seat, while Sasha and Malaika are comfortable in the backseat.

As I put it in second, Raghav pulls the hand brake and we screech to a stop. Rathore's sometimes girlfriend, Faiza, is sitting out smoking a fag and looking bored.

There's no really kind way to say this, but Faiza wasn't averse to giving it away for money. She was young and beautiful and, by all accounts, great in bed. She gave off the winey scent of heat, she knew all the little tricks, the way she licked her bee-stung lips, the way she walked. So why shouldn't she earn a little extra money to enjoy herself with?

She joins in, slipping into the backseat on the other side of Sasha. Suddenly my night is looking up. The vibe is definitely on; tonight is the night. I check her out in the rear view.

'What's up, Faiza?'

'That's not actually a question, right? You just like to listen to yourself, Zoju?'

This is what I like about Faiza. No small talk.

'Never mind this shit. Let's go get something to drink.'

The miles fly out below our wheels till at last we hit Rosie Bar, the only place where you can get booze at one in the morning. While I keep a lookout for cops, Raghav goes to the window and knocks. It opens. He hands in cash. The hand retreats and returns holding a black bag. The window closes. I'm tapping my fingers nervously on the wheel; I want to roll quickly and the sooner we're on the way, the better. The car is making me nervous. The windows don't go up, which is fine, since the AC doesn't work. The brakes are negotiable, just about, and the gearshift likes the grey areas between gears. Mileage is mood-dependent.

The CD deck in Sasha's car had long given up playing CDs, so we had jury-rigged a system with an old mp3 Discman on the dashboard, usually weighted down with a Criminal Major Acts to keep it from moving around to much. The skip protection system was fairly simple. When the front seat passenger saw bumps in the road up ahead, he would pick up the Discman and hold it firmly in his hand to soften the impact.

I gun the engine and Raghav reaches into his pocket. 'Something to wash down with our rum.' He pulls out a strip of nitros. We take a couple each. Nitrosuns are our new best friend. They're a sedative given to schizophrenics to calm them down. Ever since we found the crooked chemist in City market, nitros have accompanied the fall of night, especially once we return to hostel and can afford to be balls out nuts. For the first few minutes, it's a jitter – everything feels like a screen refreshing too fast. Lights flicker, moving objects blur, you shiver. Then reality slows down and patterns become more apparent. The moon should be only this high, the walls this red, the wind this soft: it's all in the grand scheme of things. The road is an endless perfect black ribbon of asphalt, dotted with street lamps whose light describes isosceles triangles of liquid gold. The car is driving itself, and our world is this small metal box roving the urban sea, ten eyes on an immaculate and certain future, which will realize itself tonight before dawn.

Faiza and Sasha have rolled a joint behind me, which is lit as we turn onto the flyover. Raghav hands me the bottle of Monk to keep me company as I drive, alternating it with the joint, the perfect courteous wingman. I believe I am now truly and magnificently high. Sasha and Malaika are making out and Faiza is giving Raghav a shoulder massage from behind, unbuttoning his shirt to get further. I watch jealously in the rear view mirror as Sasha puts his hand up Malaika's shirt. I should be beyond caring, but I still want to tear off a piece of what's going around. The needle is mounting steadily, and the metal is shaking, rattling, daring us to push it further, the suspension squealing. We're doing 110 now, flying over speed-breakers uncaringly. Since none of us is ready to go home quite yet, given the infinite possibility of lust and intoxication in this car, we head to the lake.

The lake is a small pond on the outskirts of Nagarbhavi, where the city decays into the countryside. The approach is through the thinning layout, where houses are increasingly more spaced out, and the road becomes dirt, then a path and then a track through a field of tall grass. Through my tunnel vision, I see the tear in the field and turn into it and slam on the brakes as we hit the slope down to the lake, then I kill the lights.

The lake is quiet, a silver shield reflecting the world above, every tree, every blade of grass and reed. There is an old temple built into the roots of the giant tree whose cover extends twenty feet over the water. We talk a bit and smoke a joint, but the call of the flesh prevents real community. Sasha and Malaika head for the far side of the tree. Raghav and Faiza head back to the car. I go with them, but Raghav indicates that my presence is undesirable. On the other side of the tree, I sit down next to Sasha and Malaika. She gives me a quick kiss and then Sasha suggests that they move further. I get the point.

So I'm drunk and stoned and horny. I lie down on a rock and look straight up at the sky, a mix of clear and clouded, all moving across the surface of the moon like a sheet being pulled off a bed.

There's this painting I'm thinking of. In the fourteenth century, this Dutch nut called Hieronymous Bosch was doing grotesque things with paint and canvas. While the whole glorious renaissance is going on in Italy and Michelangelo is envisioning the idea of a man so beautiful as to stand up and talk to God on his own terms, and Da Vinci is sketching machines to help us fly and breathe underwater, Bosch is submerged in a horrific medieval guilt trip. The 'Garden of Earthly Delights' is a tryptych on wood, and the outer two panels fold in. On the outside is a ghostly grey world, a landmass rising out of the water like a scab. The heavens are empty; there's nobody watching this channel anymore. On the inside are three pieces. There's Eden, with its creator deity, Adam and Eve and beasts both mythical and real, birds issuing out of mountains and unicorns in meadows. There's Hell with its demons, who are simulacra of all the shit you did with your life, where your insides are your outsides and you are forever devoured in a dark nightscape. And at the heart of it is the realm we live in, the Garden of Earthly Delights. Here are lovers, men riding beasts, women picking fruit, couples in caves, the asking of questions, the answering thereof, all the devices of pleasure, cavorting in the water; in short, paradise as man would have it, crowded and frenetic, with him at the heart of it. All the demons have friendly faces and open arms. There's a disquieting omnipresent symbolism. Everywhere there are fish and shellfish, the medieval symbol of the lust that drives men to perdition. Now, look carefully. You see that naked dude at the edge of the pond at the centre? That's me. I'm trapped in that garden, going around in circles, fishing, riding animals, trying to find my way back into the first picture.

Now I'm beyond lust; I'm fighting off nausea and a clenching feeling in my stomach. Everything is crowding in. A radical measure is necessary. I peel off my shirt and shorts and walk into the lake, shattering the illusion of the silver mirror. The slimy mud at the bottom mills and slips under my feet and I swallow bitter, murky water. I swim out into the centre of the filth, trying to right the spinning universe, yanking big mouthfuls out of the air. Lying on my back, breathing deeply, I'm dying for a little certainty. Half my friends are pissed at me, the other half think I'm a charity case, I've just behaved like an animal around Raghav and Sasha, and I feel only disgust.

Everywhere in the darkness, in the broken shine of the lake and the luminous pink of the city in the distance, I sense Jennifer, and I want only to lie in her lap, only to feel someone holding my head, to keep me steady, to keep me afloat. I want to turn it all back and take back all the mistakes I've made. The wrenching in my gut is either regret and melancholy, or perhaps just a cramp.

Zoju, my lad, if you could drown yourself now, it would not be ill done. They'd dredge you out of this shit, covered with slime and vermin. Then they'd beatify you as a martyr to the pressures of growing up in the modern world. Beautiful girls would cry at your funeral. Strong men would drink bitterly for months and remember you.

But I don't. I crawl out of the water, shivering and cold, my muscles cramping with fatigue. I put on my shorts and finish the last bit of rum for warmth. The sky is lightening in the distance and the college gates will be opening. On the way back, no one speaks. The early morning zombie joggers are hypnotizing, with their arm rotations and their fixed stares. Crawl into bed, surrender the ghost.

When you wake up after a night of popping nitros, you realize that you've slept far longer than you thought possible, sixteen hours maybe, and you've still gotten no rest. In a mirror, the bags under your eyes stretch down to your nostrils. The corners of your eyes are visibly stretched. You support yourself on the edge of the sink and wonder how old you look and why there's no bottom to the black wells of your pupils. It's nine at night and you want a drink. At the edge of your vision, the spirit of chaos flickers and beckons.

stranger

Noah and the Whale/
The First Days of Spring/2009

Hangover. The tongue is raspy. My head is swimming. My face doesn't feel clean; I was too dizzy to complete my toilette properly at home. I've taken two Disprins and had a litre of water. I'm drinking another litre now, glass after glass, wishing it would percolate through my system faster.

When you're hungover, the body is your prison; you cannot synthesize the outside world. The gaze turns inwards, magnifying your organs and the fluids rushing within. My belly is swollen with fat and gas, unmanageably disconnected from my skeletal system. I haven't been able to piss. Beneath my breath-mints, I smell like a tannery. The fear of people smelling it has made me spray myself down with eau de cologne and rinse with mouthwash incessantly, and still I can feel the scent of liquor leach through my hide, bubble to the surface.

Really, this is all Dhruv's fault. He lured me out last night to Retrosushi on the way out of the door.

'I was actually just thinking of going home, Dhruv. I'm a little fagged out.'

I really didn't want to go out with him. For one, when you go out with folks from work, you've got to drink a little slow, because you don't want to be plastered in front of them. For another, I had grown to hate going anywhere dressed in my work clothes. The shirt and tie and rumpled suit signal desperation and lack of choice so effectively.

'Hey bro, sleep when you're dead. You know how it is: work hard, party harder,' he said, piling the clichés high, into a giant Jenga tower of clichés perilously swaying from side to side.

I laughed uneasily and walked with him to the parking lot. His car is his pride and joy, this long white sedan with a sunroof. He's been doing EMI payments for a year and a half and has three more years pending.

'I like the sunroof.'

'You're not the only one, bro. Chicks love it. I'm like "go ahead, stick your head out of the sunroof". And all the time, I'm thinking about getting my head through her sunroof, know what I mean?'

He held his hand out for a five. I hesitated because I was just so much more disgusted than I'd thought I could possibly be. The moment grew too long and I gave him his high five. Then, because I had already given him his five, I felt bound to continue and went with him. I should have known better. Like Amlan said, if it walks like a GMPT, talks like a GMPT, sends emails like it's a GMPT, chances are that it's a GMPT.

Why would I ever voluntarily put myself in this position? And how much did I pay to hurt this badly? I tab up last night. Five hundred bucks for the ride back home. Two grand for dinner and two glasses of wine at the Pizzeria Zero. From there to Retrosushi. Martinis and manhattans at Retrosushi – eight large, the bill in my wallet says. How did I manage that alone?

As usual, I wasn't alone. The whole spinning night rises in my throat and I want to lean down between my own two knees and throw up. Rita, what are the odds her name was actually Rita? There might be only five people in the world who think her name was Rita, and three of them work on this floor. It's the sort of thing best forgotten. Who was she to everyone else at the table? Some college girl in a black dress cashing in on her youth and good looks and tautness and on the loneliness of five young guys after work. Five guys whose only need is to find a girl to laugh at their jokes, to look at them when they're talking and nod along. When I think of her, unbidden, I think of Faiza, and I think of the way she used to earn her luxuries.

I can't really recall her eyes. What I do recall is the highlights in her hair, like strands of gold, and the calculation in the tightness of her lips, the flaring of her nostrils as she sipped her Bellini and the feline pinkness of her tongue. I can remember that same tongue circling my nipples in the cab home, my shirt unbuttoned to my waist, her fingers clutching my shirt, probably weighing up the threads, her highlights bobbing down the front of my chest. The practised way she slipped one onto me. Impressionistic details in a series of dark sets. The expensive mood lighting at Retrosushi, the crooked smile of a line of coke on a wooden toilet seat, the darkness of a taxi, broken by the lights of oncoming traffic, the darkness of the staircase up to my flat, the darkness of my bedroom, the glitter on her skin. The centipede of pride crawling up my spine. Really, what colour were her eyes?

She left in the morning, taking a five hundred from my wallet for a cab. At least she was practised enough to leave no traces, apart from a scent in the sheets. She's probably sitting in some lecture hall right now, her hair pulled back in a ponytail, the makeup washed off her face. I don't think I'd be able to recognize her by daylight.

Now here's the beauty of it all. Even while I was fucking her, even while I was giving her my best, showing her the tricks I know, the swivelling of the hips, the changes in rhythm, the pinning of her hands behind her back, the show of upper body strength against the headboard, I wasn't thinking of her. I was thinking of Jennifer. I tried to stop, I really did. I did *not* want to be making love to Jennifer. I wanted to enjoy this fresh new thing, this treat life had thrown in my path. And yet, I was making love to an idea, while our bodies were out fucking. Do you ever actually sleep with the person you are sleeping with? Are you always imagining some other girl, or even that same girl at an earlier time? Is it all a thin film of fiction – a Möbius strip of experience wrapping around your mind, as your flesh creates new film, new pornography for your next assisted jack-off session?

The phone rings, and Abhilash's number flashes across the LED display. I gather my breath, let a ring pass, and pick up.

'Abhilash?'

'Zorawar, are you on this Project Zone or not?'

I rest my head on one hand. It hurts. 'Yes, Abhilash.'

'What exactly is your most basic duty on every transaction you are staffed on?'

I am silent. What have I forgotten?

'Filing, Zoju. You are supposed to file everything that comes to the group ID.'

'Yes, Abhilash. I'm filing everything in the shared folders.'

'Then,' his voice drops to a sibilant hiss, 'why haven't you saved the comments from the bankers to the business section?'

'Abhilash, I've saved it under DRHP, Business, Received from LMBs.'

'No, you haven't fucking saved them. You've saved one set of comments from them. They sent another set twenty minutes ago.'

'I'll just save it.' I hear the sound of hand sanitizer being pumped and I can see his pale digits entwining and cold with evaporating alcohol.

'It's already fucking saved, you twit. I saved it because, when I wanted it, it wasn't where it should have been. I'm just not totally clear on what you're paid to do around here.'

Click. The line is dead. I realize I'm clutching the handle so tight my knuckles are white.

What *am* I paid to do? I go to the loo, hitch up my trousers, flip my tie over my shoulder and kneel creakingly over the pot. Two fingers in the mouth, get to the uvula, here it comes. My insides convulse and I'm looking down at chunks of meat, the whiteness of flour and tomato sauces bleached by my stomach acids to a bright orange, all of it thin and smelling of booze. Repeat.

Looking at the mirror, I am shocked to see the car crash that is my face. My eyes are sunk into dark pits. The flesh sags off my cheeks, gathering near my jawline. My nostrils merge into the flesh around my mouth. I wash this brutalist sculpture.

Did I start out last night to feel like this today, to feel destroyed and unfocused, to feel cheapened and forgetful, to feel like I haven't bathed or shaved, to wonder what the name on Rita's birth certificate is?

Get back to it. Project Zone is calling. Run the comments and check the backup. That's what you're paid for. And you'd better make sure you save every damn scrap of shit that shows up in your inbox.

Later in the day, we're sitting in the conference room. The voice on the octopus phone, which has many arms, each of which has a speaker at the end, is speaking. It's the sheikh's lawyer. Our clients are a private equity group based in Dubai. Somewhere out in the desert, old money has taken the shape of new organizations, types of organizations that allow them to be even less regulated than if they just had it in mattresses.

'Well,' Abhilash says into the octopus, 'I think it's fairly clear that we fall into the approval route under FEMA 20.'

'I see,' said the voice, a voice so English and polished that you knew it came with a double-barrelled name. 'And you're saying we'd have to take permission from the Indian government for that?'

'Yes, that is correct.' Abhilash leans back. 'The process for seeking RBI approval takes approximately six weeks.'

'We can't do six weeks. Is there a way we can avoid, what is it, the RBI? Can we call it some other kind of transaction?'

'No, Jonathon. We've seen that tried, and I think it's clear that the Reserve Bank will look through to the intent of the transaction.'

Suddenly, there is a click and another voice enters the room. 'Reserve Bank?'

Jonathon doesn't miss a beat. 'Abhilash, Mr Tayyed has just joined us. He's with the Al Marah group.'

'Yes, hello.' The gruff voice is impatient. 'This Reserve Bank, it is Indian bank, yes?'

'Yes, Mr Tayyed, the Reserve Bank of India is the concerned authority.'

'And there is some problem? It will not allow us to do our deal?'

'Mr Tayyed, on the terms that we've reviewed so far, it is unlikely that we will clear it through the approval route.'

'Ok, no problem. So we buy the Reserve Bank. Then, is ok?'

Silence fills the room. Abhilash presses mute. 'Where do you even begin to explain to these people that there are things money can't buy?'

I don't know. I can't think of much that money can't buy.

When I took this job, I really didn't know what I would do with the money. I couldn't understand the ease with which people spent it. After all, a twentieth of what I was earning would be enough to live on luxuriously in college. The vast enormity of the riches I had lucked into staggered me. Besides, I thought, how would I get the time to spend it?

But you do. It's bizarre, I know, but I've stopped looking at prices. If I look at something, which is not a car or a house or really fancy electronics, and I want it, I buy it.

Enter the zinc-brushed cocktail shaker at two grand. Dinner and drinks is four large wherever you go. Genuine Arsenal jersey – two-and-a-half grand. Fancy new Sennheiser headphones – four-and-a-half grand. That's one weekend's expenditure. Then the basics. Instalment on the car – six grand. Rent – twenty grand a month. There. It's just about all gone.

How would I ever be able to earn this much money doing anything else? I'm a single-purpose machine, built to perfectly slot into this great engine, built to do deals and give comments, and it's a skill the world prizes. If I were to work anywhere *but* a law firm, I would fall behind on the most basic skills – comprehension, language skills, organizational ability.

Sometimes the realization strikes me that I have come very far from all that, that I am very much part of this world now. I like shirts with double cuffs and nice cufflinks to wear with them. I like martinis and manhattans and Belgian beers and calling cabs to take me home when all these drinks pile up. I like flying business and having people use my name when they take my coat. I like getting into clubs with cover charges and lounges smelling of cigar smoke.

Look at me. Just what's on my person. The suit cost ten grand. The shirt cost two grand. The shoes were three-and-a-half. The watch cost fifteen grand. I'm carrying thirty grand on me. Is the soft, fat despicable worm of a human being inside this rich shell worth that much?

So I get everything I want. I even save a tiny bit at the end of all that. And we're still underpaid. How do I figure, right? Where do I get off, twenty-three years old, bitching about earning almost six figures a month?

The truth is that we're a commodity. Every time I send in my timesheet and indicate who I've spent how much time working for, I'm reporting to Central Pimping, which tots up the numbers and sends out a bill to each client in seven or eight figures monthly.

They bill a first year associate's time at eight grand an hour. That's how much your clients will pay for your drafting and research. In a day, I may bill anywhere from six to sixteen hours. Effectively, I can earn the firm the equivalent of my monthly salary in a single day. My annual salary and bonus are about two weeks of my billing. Even if I stole time, stole away early every night – like Dhruv, by leaving my briefcase by my desk, my coat on my chair and my lights on – I'd still have earned it all in a month.

So buy your fancy shirts and cufflinks. Go ahead. Make down payments on your new car. Drink down that 600-buck martini. Just know that you're still being ripped off.

As the man says, money doesn't talk, it swears.

In economics, the little I remember, they call it the ratchet effect. When you get used to a certain standard of life, it becomes impossible to lower it. Conversely, raising your standard of life is just that easy – which incubates a fear in everyone who lives like this. What if I lose my job? What if I can't cut the mustard? How will I ever live on less than this much? A bitter taste fills my mouth as I voice the thought. We fear settling for less, so much so that the faster this treadmill gets, the less likely we are to get off.

I worry about it constantly. What would I do without the money? I like the things it brings me. That's how people become comfortable. They get used to it, they depend on it and then it becomes a bigger part of who they are. You get the fancy car because you can afford the down payments, get used to the foreign vacations because you can afford two weeks in a nice hotel in Spain, get used to the fancy neighbourhoods because you can handle the rent.

Then you go abroad, like Abhilash, and pick up a fancy masters degree, which plunges you into a netherworld of hard-currency debt. You have to work a couple of years in a foreign law firm to pay off the loans and, before you know it, you're thirty-two and you've been doing transactions so long that it's all you know. Somewhere along the way, you got married and had yourself a kid and, now, there's no way to turn your back on this world. The doors that were open have shut themselves behind you. Your only friends are lawyers and bankers, bankers and lawyers, wankers and thieves, the only places you feel welcome in cater to lawyers and bankers. Now, even if you wanted to, you wouldn't be able to change a thing. Slowly your world consumes you, and you develop a sense of pride about how much you have given. Abhilash tells the story of his son's birth often, over team drinks. While his wife was screaming and convulsing in the delivery ward, Abhilash was in the waiting room, with his phone and his laptop, negotiating a closing. He's very proud of the fact that he *closed two deals* that day.

In every man who thinks recreationally, there's some quantum of desire to learn from the pain of others. See the aged, the infirm, the dead – all in one chariot-ride around this floor. What do I see on my grand tour? I see the overweight, the obsessively tense and stressed, the cynical, the lonely, the BlackBerry addicts.

They're actually so young. No one on this floor is older than forty. At forty, you could be in your prime as a man.

Think of Odysseus. He must have been at least twenty before he set sail for Troy. The war wound on for ten years, before Troy burnt like a beacon in the Mediterranean. The voyage home, with its enchantresses, monsters and vicious sirens took another ten years. So, when Odysseus came home to his island kingdom in disrepair and his hall full of suitors to his wife, he must have been about forty years old. At that age, he dressed up as an old beggar, walked through the pillars of his hall, through their scornful eyes, picked up his old bow, the bow no one else could even string, and fired an arrow through the loops of eleven axes. Then he locked the doors of the palace and killed every single one of them and took back his wife and his throne.

Will any of these guys be able to pull off such a singular act of badassery at forty? Will they, my ass. At forty, they'll be paying the gardener to fuck their wives for them. Chances are, they'll be paying extra to watch.

famous blue raincoat

Leonard Cohen/Songs of Love and Hate/1971

This is it then: the half-dream, half-nightmare. The unutterable mistake.

We are in a room in the heart of the old town, in Kiran's brother's flat. Kiran, Jennifer and I are sitting around on an old yellow mattress on the floor. The sun is white through the yellow curtains and everything is drenched in buttery warmth. There are rum bottles in the corner and one of them has a little left. I am trying to work up the energy to get to it and pour, but my desire is poisoned by the knowledge that there is no more Coke, so it'll have to be rum and tap water and it is just too early for that. We're all looking a little jangled and wasted. One of the Batman movies is playing on the desktop in the corner. Liam Neeson is wearing a black Ninja outfit.

Amlan has just left, saying he has some work to submit. I suspect he has left because this looks like a crime scene and he wants to exonerate himself. Soon I too will leave, to meet Sasha, who wants to see some play reading at a defunct mechanic's garage. He had met the playwright at the RTO in Benson Town. There really was not a spare joker in the world Sasha did not have time to entertain. It seemed also that all of the world's spare jokers magically knew this.

'Zoju, do we have any more fags?'

I reach for the pack in the corner. The top has been ripped off to make roaches and there is half a cigarette rattling about at the bottom.

'Nothing.' Liam Neeson echoes my disappointment. Christian Bale is bent over on the floor. He has much to learn.

'Get some, na?'

'No. I don't want to smoke. You do. You get it.'

'Fuck, what a guy.'

'Go, be a big man. Face the sunlight and neighbours and traffic and go get fags.'

'Ok, I'll get them. But if you guys smoke even one, I'll kill you.'

Kiran finds his slippers and shuts the door behind him. Now, it's just Jenni and me. We sprawl next to each other on the mattress and watch Batman being trained in some monastery. I am lying behind her. I see the screen through the gentle curve of her side, a basin of blue T-shirt. Batman executes moves in the monastery, then he executes them in the streets of Gotham. We are expected to congratulate ourselves on spotting the parallel.

I put my hand up to Jennifer's hip and rest on it, ostensibly moving it down to get a better view. She snuggles down a bit, her shirt riding up her hip a little. I see the top of her underwear, and recognize it, the yellow high cut with the bow on the front. Because I have leant forward and she has turned back a little, we are now closer than we were. Out of some kind of muscle memory, I move forward a little and now we are spooning.

We lie like this for a little bit. My nose is too close to her neck. I am hard against the hollow of her back. I reach up and smooth some of her hair back. Her eyes close. There is a silence that you can breathe, a non-invitation in the air. I rest my hand on her hip. It is all right, we are friends. This is permitted. Men and women are only ever this kind of friends, their friendship is always in the shadow of a loaded gun.

Then my hand moves up, and it is not gliding, it is gripping, and then it is grasping and she is not wearing a bra. Jennifer mewls and turns her head. The silence is shattered like a mirror, its shards are strewn across the yellow mattress.

We kiss hungrily, our tongues searching and probing, reexamining each other. No longer are we thinking about the knock on the door. My hand is under her shirt and her nipples are as I remember them, brown and hard. She is unzipping me, and there is urgency. She is whispering into my ear, 'Quickly, Zoju.'

She holds my head and tells me again not to think about it. I sink into her and it's wet and warm and I am home. I am not thinking about the knock on the door.

I move in her furiously and she locks her legs behind my back, and she's trying not to think of the knock on the door. I am thrusting and am thrusting too fast, too urgently in the warmth of her, and not thinking about the knock on the door.

Suddenly, we are both thinking of the fact that there is no knock on the door. I lose control and she squirms out from under me. I come awkwardly, half on her back and on the yellow mattress, both of us half-naked in the yellow light. My abdomen is convulsing and I am spewing, but I am only thinking of the door and of Kiran who will knock on the door.

She laughs, 'You were never so quick when we were together, Zorawar.' And then she runs into the bathroom. I put my pants back on and try to scrape the jizz off the mattress. Then I poke my head into the bathroom, and she is cleaning up, and her brown legs are beautiful against the white tiles on the wall, and she is crying.

'I love him. I love him so much. I can't believe I just did this.' She sobbed. 'I hate girls who do this kind of thing. He's such a good guy, he's such a great guy. He loves me so much and I love him too.'

I rest my head against the door. 'I'm sorry. I shouldn't have ...'

She turns and looks at me, 'You didn't rape me, Zoju. You're just a bad friend.'

I look away, at the door on which there has been no knock. 'I'm a terrible friend.'

Now she has dried her eyes, and she is laughing, she is laughing with joy. 'Zoju, I thought I still loved you, but I don't! I don't love you at all. I love him. I love him so much and I am sure of it for the first time.'

She puts on her pants and we sit down. Somehow, a reckoning has taken place. This is over. It is over forever. I am relieved; no harm has come of it. Now we can continue and this will all be just past, just pleasant memories.

There is a knock on the door. I open it. Kiran is holding a pack of fags and two plastic bags.

'I got you ungrateful idiots breakfast. Idlis and sambar.'

I feel like I am falling into a hole somebody has placed behind me like in a cartoon. Jennifer jumps up and runs to him, takes the packets from him and hugs him and then kisses him on the cheek.

'Wow. They're only idlis.'

Kiran lights a cigarette and sits down. Then he points at the screen, 'Isn't this so predictable? How Liam Neeson is the bad guy all along?'

If only that had been the end of it.

good fortune

P.J. Harvey/Songs from the City, Songs from the Sea/2000

Things had gotten better for Amlan as they got worse for the rest of us. For one, he got jaundice. It was the best thing ever to happen to him. Through teeth-chattering high temperature and system failure, he lost twenty kilos and got in shape. Suddenly, there was the whirlwind acquisition of a new wardrobe, new jeans, white muscle shirts, Converse sneakers. Then he got a second-hand bike, which could now take his weight and then, because he was finally ready, he started the search for someone to ride pillion.

One afternoon shortly before exams, Kelkar and I were on our third coffee, which means we had spent an hour sitting on the steps. Amlan pulled up on his rat bike extraordinaire, the light-framed Yamaha Rx 100. He walked to the Five Buck Shop window and bought two small Gold Flakes. The first he tucked behind his ear, letting his hair hold it in place. The second he placed between his lips and lit with a match from the small jar in the counter, striking it against the matchbox tied to the shutter. Then exhaling, he walked to us.

'Guys, there's someone I want you to meet.'

This was meat to us.

'Too good.'

'Finally.'

'Tell us more.'

'Does she only use her mouth to breathe?'

'Is she over sixteen?'

'Prehensile tail?'

'Above or below eighty kilos?'

Amlan looked down at us, opened his mouth as if to say something, then thought the better of it. He inhaled, exhaled and then walked to his bike.

'I think I'll let you guys just see this yourselves. I'll be meeting Nicki at Pecos tonight. Come if you want.'

He kicked the start and rode off. It started without a key. You just had to clutch and kick and it would cough into life. Kiran used to take advantage of that for chai trips in the middle of the night.

Kelkar sat up with a start. 'Bastard! He's done it! I knew it. The tasteful white T-shirts, the haircut. He's nailing some model.'

'Nicki.' I worked out the problem. 'Nikita? Nicole? Nicola? Nicolletta? French or Italian or Spanish? Russian? What the hell has he managed to land himself?'

Kelkar was beside himself. 'He's going to rub our faces in it. I know it. She'll be six feet tall and here for Lakme Fashion Week or something, and she'll have huge sunglasses and high heels and a little dress.'

'Boss, even by your own suspicions, a model, not a porn star.'

In the auto, all the way to Pecos, we constructed Nicola. She was a brunette, at Kelkar's insistence. I gave her a limp – something to be shy about, a left leg two inches shorter than the right one, like Garrincha.

'That way she can't be doing ramp work, but she's still fine for print work.'

'Also, she can't be doing ramp work because she's not that tall. I mean, she can't be more than two inches taller than Amlan.'

'Maybe she's got a history, like, a past she's running away from.'

'Or that she's ashamed of. Maybe she's like ... a dairy farmer's daughter from Brescia.'

'Who was spotted at a farm fair by a scout. From the mozzarella stand to Milan in one week.'

'In fact, Amlan's probably got her convinced he's Oriya royalty and, therefore, a leg up in the world.'

'I'm not sure how much of a leg up that *could* be.'

'Must be better than churning milk all day in a windowless shed.'

We got to Pecos. The grimy window outdoors rattled. Men walked in and out of the slot machine saloon below. In we went, through the narrow door, waving at the bartender who was pulling a heady pitcher under the giant mushroom poster. The sound system was playing Traffic. Some bourgeois assface in work clothes in the corner was actually requesting 'Smoke on the Water'. Hip, dude. With it. I gave him a thumbs up. He smiled gratefully. Asswipe.

At our table in the corner, Amlan was sitting with Sasha and some Mallu-looking dude with shoulder-length hair.

There was a pitcher on the table and a plate of chilly beef with mostly chillies left. Amlan had *that* look on his face.

'Haan,' Kelkar said, as he slid onto the bench next to Sasha. 'So, where's Nicki?'

Sasha giggled into his beer. The Mallu guy straightened up and said, 'I'm Nicki.'

Silence for a moment. I clarify, 'No, the Nicki you wanted us to meet, Amlan.'

Amlan thumbed left. 'That's Nicki.'

Sasha was practically blowing bubbles into his beer with joy. 'Guys, in case you still somehow don't get it, Amlan's coming out.'

My mind was agog with the wrongness of what was happening. Clearly this was all a put-on. No one was straighter than Amlan. He smoked dirty cigarettes and rode a dirt bike. He lived in a room so dirty that you were never sure if what you were standing or sitting on was lunch or dinner. His ashtray was a flowerpot that overflowed constantly. His cupboard had colonies of spiders living in it. He bathed once or twice a week. He liked *Trainspotting* and *Pulp Fiction* and *Reservoir Dogs* and *A Fistful of Dollars*. His favourite artists were Rage Against the Machine, Led Zeppelin and David Bowie. How could he possibly be a fairy?

'But you're not gay.'

Amlan was thoughtful. 'No, well, I don't know about *gay*, but I like boys.'

Well, maybe the David Bowie should have tipped me off.

Kelkar was desperate. 'But you like girls also, don't you? You do. You liked Zeenat Aman in *Satyam Shivam Sundaram*? You have that poster of Cindy Crawford up on your cupboard? You like girls just fine!'

Amlan, meditatively, 'Girls are okay I guess, but boys …'

'… are so firm and beautiful, no?' interjected Sasha. 'They're so linear and rational and their company is so fraternal and equal.'

Kelkar turned, red-eyed. 'What, you too?'

'Nope. He just talks like that,' I said to calm him. 'Every morning.'

Nicki looked at us like he was calculating his chances of getting out alive, wondering if he would make it to the stairs before Kelkar or some other psycho nailed him. I decided to diffuse the tension somehow.

'So, anyway, Nicki. What is it you do?'

Sasha, helpfully, 'Besides Amlan.'

Kelkar was not letting this go. 'Okay, so assuming, but not conceding, that you're not just having us on, which one of you, you know, gets on top?'

'Gentlemen don't tell.'

Kelkar couldn't take it any longer. He got up and walked away, yelling as he went, 'What a load of shit! Why don't you wolfbag each other till you can't shit straight anymore?'

Nicki, who I was starting to realize was a little high-strung, started and his eyes grew wide. The old dudes in the corner didn't react. All this sodomy and violence was a young man's game.

'What's wolf *banging*?'

Sasha, helpful, 'Wolfbagging.'

'Never mind him,' I tried to cover, 'he's a little conservative. He'll come around. Now tell us about yourself.'

Maybe Kelkar thought this was all a big wheeze; maybe he was let down because Nicki wasn't a poor Italian milkmaid on the make. But I had no doubts myself. Looking at Amlan, then Nicki, and back at Amlan in disbelief, I knew. Love is that thing that can impart a glow to even Amlan, our very own Prince of Darkness.

As I listened to Nicki tell us about the world of fashion design and his projects, and watched Amlan look at him indulgently, I felt something turn a little in my guts. I had always thought that I was luckier than Amlan, luckier in temperament, athleticism, even ability. More than anything, I was so sure that I was luckier than him in love. After all, I was getting more action than I had ever dreamt of in my masturbatory youth. But the way Amlan looked at Nicki, just that little bit of indulgence, kindness and protectiveness, caused something in me to kink slightly.

When we left Pecos at night, a little dizzy, a little coloured, I walked ahead with Amlan and Sasha was chatting Nicki up about female pop artists, and telling him Toni Braxton's 'Unbreak My Heart' had changed his life. Then he put his arm around Nicki's shoulders, as we steered into the crowd, 'See, now, *wolf*bagging ...'

crown of love

Arcade Fire/Funeral/2004

We're in Abhilash's office, with all the deal toys on the desk and the windowsill. Little plastic tombstones, cutesy souvenirs from bond issues, preferential capital issues. A tiny plastic aeroplane on a stand from an aviation re-financing. Bankers spend the time that they're not on their Berries designing deal toys to gift themselves. When he's feeling thoughtful, I've seen Abhilash pick up the little plane and fly it across his desk.

Today, he's not thoughtful. We're in trouble. I'm standing against the doorframe, while Dhruv is leaning with both hands on a chair.

'Zorawar, Dhruv.' He pumps sanitizer onto his palm and starts rubbing his hands together. 'Why did you send out our opinion on Zone?'

I look at Dhruv. He had told me to send it half an hour ago. Kicked at the opportunity, I drafted out a snappy email and mailed the opinion to the whole group. Dhruv looks back at me.

'Zorawar sent it out. I'm not sure why.'

The bastard. The slimeball. The cocksucker. What a GMPT. What do I do? I can't contradict him without proof. Do I cover for him and play the hand I've been given? Or do I try to brazen it out on my word? Abhilash has put his head between his hands and the voice is coming from the cavern of his palms.

'Why?'

My voice trips over my tongue on its way out. 'I thought you'd already reviewed it and it would be okay. Morgan Stanley were calling and pressuring me.'

'Of course they would be pressuring you.' It's almost a groan, from deep within the cavern. Dhruv's a spectator now – I've taken the bait and this is now my screaming. Abhilash's face pops out of his hands, his eyes red with rage and lack of sleep. 'They're fucking bankers. It's their job profile. They're paid to get the deal done. Are you a banker, Zorawar?'

Abhilash uses the word *banker* as an explosive, like all the consonants can't get out his mouth fast enough.

'No, Abhilash.'

'That's right, you're not. Congratulations – awareness dawns. You're not a banker. You're a lawyer.' Lawyer comes out elongated, a slide down to the indeterminacy at the end. 'As a lawyer, your problem is that these sons of bitches are fundamentally too cheap to pay you. You're not trying to get the deal done. At this stage, you're trying to ensure we get paid. Everything's filed, so the only thing you still have in your power is our fucking legal opinion.' He laughs bitterly. 'Which you've given away without us getting paid. You know what you're like, Zorawar?'

'No, Abhilash.'

'You're like a girl on the marriage market. It's two days before your engagement and you've let him fuck you in the back of his car. Now he can walk out on you and you're screwed. In this analogy, you see, Zorawar, the hero is the guy who's got what he wanted out of you without having to give you your prize, much like this banker's fucked us. And you're here, trying to explain to your mom how nice he was to you.'

Abhilash starts firing his sharp, bitter laugh at me. 'Did you let him buy you a nice drinkie, Zorawar? Something pink, with an umbrella in it?' Dhruv joins him in it. The GMPT has flipped me over and is giving it to me for all he's worth.

Then the laughter cuts out and he leans forward. Abhilash's eyes are blazing red, ringed with their perpetual dark circles, firepits against his pale, bloodless face. 'The banks are your clients. Whom do you WORK for?'

'The firm.' It comes out uncertain and weaker than I would have liked. My vocal cords are dry.

'Damn straight. Now I'm going to have to call that fucker's boss and convince him we need to be paid even though you've thrown your pretty legs up in the air.'

Silence.

'Get out!' he screams. I leave. Dhruv comes out behind me.

'Zorawar,' he says quietly. I stop. He's going to apologize to me. Fine, I'll say it's cool, never mind. I'll take a bullet for you, man. It's all good. 'Zorawar, it's okay. We all make mistakes. Don't worry about it. He's a screamer – it's okay, you get a screaming bonus at the end of the year for taking it like a man.'

I'm speechless, apoplectic. This is the ultimate GMPT move; the semen-soaked handkerchief across the face. It's like the sound is on mute and all I can see is his mouth moving, the little drop of wetness at the corner of his mouth. The sound I hear in my ears is a wall of rushing waves, the blood pumping in my neck. I would be forgiven for punching him, right?

But something stops me. It's the familiar slowness and coldness in my body. Would anyone buy my side of it now? It's not the done thing, right? We all wear ties and shirts and our complaints come out as emails. It's the professional thing to do. Mark the name partner of the firm and let the system work for you. Nobody here is your friend. From the other party's counsel down to the body directly above you, everyone is just a different kind of enemy – a set of interlocking enemies, whom you can use one against the other, in turn, to deflect blame, to protect yourself and your bonus.

Would Sasha have let Dhruv and Abhilash walk over him the way I have today? No way. He'd embarrass himself yelling out the truth, his face turning red with indignation. He might have quit today. In fact, word in the industry would probably have been that he was unemployable. His courage would have made him a lunatic – unfit to mingle, to engage in the give-and-take, to surrender to the positional thinking of the corporate world.

He just wasn't made to survive in this world. My world is one of bullies and yes men. Of turning the other cheek, of turning it so far that you turn 180 degrees and bend over till you can smell your own ass. To survive, you must never put yourself in a position where you will be expected to turn.

I look around. I fit into this world. If I am prudent enough, I'll make sure that I always cover my ass. I'll run any questions past Abhilash. I'll mark him on any mails I send to Dhruv. If I get it down on paper, I'll minimize the screamings I get. When you live in this world, you learn its ways.

But above all of the positional thinking and the calculation of costs, beyond all rational doubts, is that numbing doubt about whether I'd actually connect if I threw a punch. What if I miss, or don't hit him hard enough? God knows I've never actually hit someone first, or hard enough.

After all, I didn't act that day, when I should have, the day everyone jumped in and I stayed out. It was, as usual, Sasha's fight to begin. He had come down the Nagarbhavi slope in his car, in the afternoon. Then the Portuguese man came out of the side gali between Surya and the State Bank of India, his scooter laden with coconuts. Sasha braked hard and swerved, but still hit the front wheel of the scooter. The man took a tumble, his coconuts rolling freely down the hill. Sasha, being that *special* kind of moron, stepped out and started berating the guy for driving carelessly. Huge mistake, because the Portuguese who had gathered saw only an arrogant outsider in a car, who had hit one of theirs, on a two wheeler, no less. Instead of begging for forgiveness and picking up the coconuts, the North Indian had the temerity to start jawing with him.

A Portuguese crowd gathered, baying for blood. From Law School, the chillers at Five Buck Shop were the first up the street. People left afternoon seminars. The post-lunch crowd at hostel tried to grab rides to get there faster. At the same time, the entire afternoon drinking crowd of Surya

Bar had stepped out; drunk, unemployed, irascible. Faced with this incredibly explosive mix, Sasha still doggedly and loudly protested that the fault was not his. Just as the first twenty people came over the hill, the first stone was thrown. Thereby began the first riot in Nagarbhavi's recorded history.

The police surrounded the area and, predictably, started whacking everyone in sight, student and Portuguese bar drunk equally. In the middle of it all was Sasha, his shirt torn off. Everyone was in the melee, Amlan without his glasses, swinging wildly and ineffectively, Raghav standing on the far side of the car trying to get the cops to stop the right people. Wild knots formed and disappeared like eddies in a river. Focal points appeared everywhere, but the white 800 drew the most people. Chunks of stone from the divider hit the car, landing in the backseat, shattering the windshield. The battle raged wildly out of control until the cop patrols showed up in force and started arresting people.

How did I have this bird's eye view of everything? Because I was at the top of the hill, frozen in fear. My blood ran cold, a giant ball of dirty street ice forming in my belly, forbidding motion. My body was full of inaction, unable to move forward or back, unable to help my friends and yet unable to walk away from the scene. It plays itself out in my head over and over. I see everything move so slowly.

I helped take the car away to the service station. I helped people to the hospital. I did what I could. But, at the end of the day, there's no way around it: I pussied out of the fight. I could feel it in the way everyone looked at me afterwards, appraising me, examining every ounce of muscle on me and then writing it off as a non-performing asset. That night, after everyone had been stitched up and iced off, and had made their statements to the cops, they all sat on the terrace with a bottle of whisky and told war stories to each other, told each other how it looked to them, talked about the size of the rock they found in the back seat, passed around the piece of glass the doctor dug out of Raghav's thigh.

Kelkar and Amlan went to a side of the terrace, I was later told by Sasha. They spoke for a while and they hugged, and everything between them was as it always was. They had bled together in combat and now they were brothers again. The only one who didn't count for shit was me.

I sat in the library, forcing myself through some insurance law, reading about risk and reward. Every word I read confirmed the calculated wisdom of my decision. My premiums would always stay low. The contract of insurance is one against accident, I read, not one that exists to subsidize those who call danger upon themselves. The law protects the prudent. When the library closed for the night, I went back to my hostel and straight to my room. I left the door open for Sasha and lay down on my bed to think about the day. Through the window, I could hear the conversation from the terrace – the laughter of the brave.

The excoriation of the brave man, of the pity he feels for you – that is the real punishment of the coward. Every time I think about that day, I am ashamed of my inaction, ashamed that I did not jump into the fray.

I suppose it was worse because of how close I was to Sasha. He was stupidly brave. If he saw the right in something, he'd be blind to everything else. Maybe if he was more like me, he'd be alive today. He'd have apologized to the voices in the dark and let the moment pass. He'd have graduated and be working in Bombay or Delhi, like he was supposed to.

But danger is everywhere. It lurks in sunlit places, in happy times. It can coil up like a snake and strike at will. Looking back, it's evident that we all went down far more perilous roads than we had expected to. Some unstated rule decrees that once you've started on the long road down, you must wait to be derailed, something must happen to knock you off your path.

After class, when we bothered to go at all, we'd end up at Rathore's place. Away from hostel and secrecy, and the segregation of sexes, we found a sort of proxy home. Rathore's pad was a pink house with a front gate, three rooms and a terrace. Unencumbered by a landlord or neighbours, it really was a castle. Rathore lived there with Faiza. He should have graduated two years earlier, but could you blame him for abandoning ambition to pursue such a low paradise?

The house reeked of drugs. The door was always open and you could go right in. Rathore would be on a couch in front of the telly, stroking his bulldog, joint in hand. The stuff was in a carved-wood supari case. The supari case was his grandfather's, carved out of teak when Burma was still part of India and Rathore's grandfather was a feudal landlord in Bihar. I guess Rathore's grandfather wouldn't really have minded his supari case full to the brim with fibrous green weed; it might have appealed to the maker of grand gestures in him.

Faiza would be curled up on a mattress in a bra and a pair of shorts, her smooth pale body devoured by the eyes of visitors. But Faiza didn't mind. That day, Faiza was wearing a red spaghetti strap top and asleep on a couch in Rathore's lap. Really peaceful. They weren't always like that. When they used to fight, it used to get physical pretty often. Given how skinny Rathore was, it was an even match, so the bruises used to be fairly distributed. They'd swing from hitting each other to doing hilariously domestic things in the space of minutes.

Raghav and I were out on a mattress, preparing to do lines of ketamine. Rathore had just managed to wangle a box of vials off his crooked chemist in the old city. We cooked it in a spoon over the stove in the kitchen, the liquid bubbling and then turning white. Slowly it all evaporated, leaving only the gritty white powder. We scraped it off, made lines with a card and snorted them up through a hundred-rupee note. Because Rathore approached drugs the way Olympic athletes approach time trials, he disdained the practice of snorting ket. He pushed a syringe into a vial and tapped out the air bubbles carefully, and then, having located a visible vein in his thigh, injected himself. The little blood that drew back into the syringe, he sprayed out onto the floor next to him.

Ket puts you out of the world as a functioning human. Your mind is aware of the world as a lit place far away as you tumble into darkness. Reality exists at the end of a long cool tunnel, and it is always somebody else's business. Time recuses itself. The disconnect between body and mind is total. After twenty minutes, the extreme inertia disappears, but you're zoned out all day.

I saw it happen through that tunnel. Rathore was glassy-eyed on the couch, his syringe next to his thigh. Then suddenly, he started convulsing. Blood spurted from his nose and I remember thinking that a vessel must have burst. But I could do nothing. Rathore thrashed on the floor like a jellyfish, knocking over beer bottles and panting. It could have been seconds, or years.

Raghav stood up, paranoid. He ran to the door and shut it quickly, yelling, 'Shut up, you fucker! Shut up and stop it!' He drew the curtains, peering behind them to ensure that no one had seen anything. Faiza lay back, holding her head and moaning. I was trying to get up, slow as a zombie. Rathore had bled all over the floor and was covered in the thick red of arterial blood. He had stopped thrashing, but he was gasping and his chest was heaving.

Luckily, we had all forgotten about Kelkar who had come to collect a project from my laptop and was upstairs going through it. He came down and took in the scene. Then he said, 'I'm going to call an ambulance.' Raghav shouted, 'No! No docs! No cops! There are too many drugs in here!'

'He'll die! God knows what he's on!'

'He's just having a reaction. Let him be. He'll be fine.'

Kelkar grabbed Rathore and headed for the door, the limp bloodied body over his shoulder, eyes rolling. I was crouching by the door and I saw Raghav heading to hit him, but I was mute. Raghav gathered up all the strength the ket had left him and hit him on the back of the head, but most of his arm connected with Rathore. Kelkar turned around, the volcano exploded and out poured all the magma of his anger, contempt and frustration. He only hit Raghav four times, but it was enough to leave him lying on the floor gasping. He put Rathore in Raghav's car, and dragged me jittering and gibbering into the harsh daylight. I gulped, dry throated. He slapped me twice, hard, stinging, bruising slaps, and dragged me up by my collar. 'What are you doing, Zoju? What are you doing to yourself?' he hissed. 'Are these the people you want to become?'

I turned and fell to the ground and, through my churning brain, I saw what he saw in his anger, myself in the picture. A whore on a mattress. A coward who'd rather let his friend die than risk the cops. A blood-covered junkie with a death wish.

'No,' I pushed the word through my throat, which was dry with fear. I was scared of Kelkar who was blocking out the sun. 'It's not my fault.'

Kelkar kicked me in the chest, and I sensed his anger roil and roister. It bubbled fiercely out of him, his dislike of Rathore, of Raghav, of the culture of lying around on couches and falling out of the universe. He kicked me again. I was sure I heard something snap in my chest.

'It's not my fault. Why are you kicking me?' I believed it. It wasn't my fault. I was high, and the potted plants smelt like wet death and the pink paint of the house was fading before my eyes. I couldn't stand up. Why couldn't he understand that I was zoned?

He kicked me again, hard in the ribs. It hurt even through the numbness of the ketamine.

'How the fuck is it not your fault what you put in your body, you fucking junkie? Who held a fucking gun to your head and made you get stoned, huh?'

He shoved me into the car to hold Rathore and keep talking to him. We took him to the emergency, where they defibrillated him and then they put the long tube down his throat and pumped out his stomach, and all the pills he had taken came out, half dissolved, with the dyes that made them red and pink and blue still on them. I helped as much as I could, suddenly more sober than I thought I could have been. Rathore weighed forty-eight kilos – forty-eight kilos at nearly six feet – after they pumped his stomach, a skeleton with skin on a white sheet. His parents came down in the evening and, when he opened his eyes, he did not know who they were.

After Rathore's parents had taken over at the hospital, I stepped outside. Only the faintest hazy penumbra of my trip remained. The sky was turning to night, the deep bruise purple of the end of the sunset was ablaze in the west, above the coconut trees. My left side ached bitterly and was tender. Suddenly I felt a sense of slipping, like a direction had been revealed to me.

Where was I going? Would I ever end up as hooked as Rathore? Unlikely. But I was becoming more and more like him, circling an emptiness of drugs and meaninglessness. I hadn't gone running in months. I had no idea how my grades were. I hadn't cleaned my room or paid my bills or done anything that would have been the maintenance of a normal, productive life. It was April and I couldn't remember a clear thing since last September. Half a year of my life had disappeared into nothing.

Rathore went to rehab for two months and then came back and kept doing whatever he felt like. He and Faiza moved even further from college and were seen there even less.

And I took the exit I saw. I went back to college and begged Jennifer to take me back, to save me from everything out there, all the evil in little tablets and needles, the darkness in the lonely night, the lack of touch with reality, all the evil that people will do to themselves. I told her I missed her, that my life was tied around her in an endless complex weave. I told her that I would do anything to have her back – and at that moment, I swear, I would have.

When I think about the days that followed, the first thing I see is Kiran driving halfway to Mysore, to his brother's place, hunched over the handlebars of his bike, crying into his helmet.

I've known Kiran long enough to have seen him cry more than once. I saw him cry when we cremated Sasha. I saw him cry when I helped him pack his bags to go home when his dad had a heart attack.

It rained furiously that day, the monsoons raking across the land, an electric storm tearing up the sky, and Jenni was wearing a green men's shirt and shorts, and the rain had soaked it onto her like one long changing and glistening fish-skin. The quad was empty of people, they were huddled around the sides in the darkness – the lights had gone. That night, I told her what I thought was the truth. On my knees I swore it. That my world had mapped all its functions to her, to this one gravitational centre, that there was a centre missing to my orbits. That love is usage and syntax, and without her, it was now a ragged lace fringe around a large nothing. I honestly don't know why I said all that, because it wasn't all true. Maybe, I just hadn't tried hard enough and so I kept returning to the urge of the lodestone. I was tired of the cold desert and hungry for love that wasn't a passing sensation, and I would have said anything to feel safe.

We talked and we held each other, the rain kept falling, electric on our skins, forcing the issue. We walked down the flagstone path, through the world washed and created anew and Edenic, the mud splashing our legs.

When the rain was over and the lightning had stopped flashing and just the effort of being out in that weather had exhausted us, Jennifer took me back. She stood against the tree at the edge of the basketball court, soaked and blending in to the knobbed bark. I stood a step lower so we could see eye to eye.

Turning and looking through the ferns of this new Mesozoic, I told her that this was all I wanted, and that this time it would work. But there was sadness in her eyes and someone, somewhere, was losing something.

the killing moon

Echo and the Bunnymen/Ocean Rain/1984

It's the first of October. Every other day of the year, I can handle it. I dismiss the darker memories and celebrate his life, remembering all the times we had together. I think of him as the silent partner in conversations, ready to listen to me talk about anything. I like to run things by him and check the course of my actions against the touchstone of his courage and integrity and childish commitment to not stopping for anything.

But on this one day, none of that works. I still haven't gotten out of bed and all I want is someone to hold me. There are only a handful of people who could hold me and comfort me today, and none of them is here. Maybe I will always be like Frodo, ice gnawing the bones of my shoulder, the evil spreading outward and dimming the light every October after Weathertop. We are like no other species, human beings, in that we can be chilled by the past. Deer don't turn to stone at the memory of headlights. Foxes don't perk up their ears at the memory of a crack in the dark. But we do. Memories drive us to act or, as I am doing so completely today, not act.

I called in sick and told the HR manager that I had food poisoning. He laughed knowingly, sensing a hangover, and told me to get well soon. I wanted to reach through the radio waves and grab him by the jowls and slap the significance of the day into him.

It happened in the fall, that long decline from summer to winter. Now that it is done, I can see it clearly foretold, like a prophecy, like those webs the spiders spun.

All year, we had watched the large spiders. They were beautiful, coloured like a pack of highlighters, with long elegant black legs like a concert pianist's fingers. They were the size of a hand and fiercely carnivorous. Suspended at angles to the ground, they swam between the trees that lined the path to the men's hostels. Their webs layered the air, in all directions. Any poor beetle or fly that entered was certain prey, because the silk maze had no exits. That is how they hunted him.

Afterwards, everyone blamed the economy and the politics for the xenophobia. The escalating violence, the harsh looks, the careless protection of the police – they should have served as warnings. There had been three fights in the past month alone in Nagarbhavi after dark. They all followed the same pattern. A tiny trigger set off a disagreement. A Portuguese mob gathered quickly, surrounding the outsiders. They started demanding money. Then they proceeded to beat the outsiders up. When the police arrived, they would ask what you were doing here in the first place, not being Portuguese. The assholes spent the night in the hole and went home the next morning. Going to Surya had become hazardous.

It was the last night of the trimester before the break. I was at Surya with Jennifer and we were having one of those evenings of poisonous silence. 'I don't want to be here. You drink too much.'

'You just don't like her.'

I motioned to Malaika, who had just shown up with Sasha, who in turn looked like he was cooking up some devilry. There were half a dozen people who had been there long enough to be juiced up for anything, and the closing of Surya was not likely to be the end of the night.

'I don't like her. She's disgusting. And I want to go.'

'Come on,' I said weakly. 'Have another.'

'I'm leaving,' she said. Because she was leaving, and it was late, I walked out behind her. I told Sasha I'd see him in the room and walked back down the road, around the mud of the construction, which was wet and clung to my chappals. I was drunk enough not to care, yet more sober than I wanted to be.

In the hostel, I was filling up a bottle of water at the cooler when I got an unpunctuated message from Raghav that Sasha had run into trouble again. Thinking this would turn out to be just another punch-up with the Portuguese, which would be all sorted out by the time I got there, I ran up the street towards Surya, outside which all the recent trouble had taken place. But Amlan overtook me on his bike and shouted, 'At the lake.' A lump of ice formed in my belly. Jumping on the bike, we rode down the dark road to the lake, made lumpy by the rain. The tableau that awaited us is seared into my head. The white 800 is parked on the side of the road, and Raghav is clutching his leg and moaning in front of it. Faiza is catatonic in the front seat. Sasha is bleeding generously, his head in Malaika's lap. There is dark blood in the muddy puddles, and it is not thin blood, like water, but thick blood, like tissue and gore. His eyes are wide open.

They say death is many things; living people speaking of things they could never know. What they never mention is how heavy death actually is. I carried Sasha into the hospital, and I already knew he was dead by the way he lay limp and slack in my arms, his head bent backwards, eyes unseeing. The stab wounds in his neck and chest were so geometrical, neat like slots you could put a coin into, and there was no blood rushing out anymore. His skin was cold and clammy in the rain. I put him on a gurney and waited with Amlan. We stood outside in the drizzle and then the doctor came out and asked us who was the closest to Sasha. When he told me, I was ready.

I went to the parking bay on the side of the hospital and called Sasha's dad. I cut the call and stared at the white light and the patterns it made on the iron grates and pipes, realizing that I did not know the words for what I had to say, that no language had words for what I had to say. I turned back to the phone – this was the one time life demanded that I be a man. I redialled and, when Sasha's father picked up, I took a deep breath and told him. The old soldier heard me, asked if I was sure and then thanked me, saying he was sending someone over.

The crowd that had gathered outside the hospital held each other and cried, an impromptu wake. They cried through that night for the handsome young corpse on the metal bed inside, his eyes open, staring into something they couldn't see, his lips loose and open.

'You should have been with him,' sobbed Jennifer, holding my shirt. 'I should have let you stay.'

'Don't be an idiot. I wasn't going to go for that drive anyway,' I said, but what I wondered was, if I had been there, *would I have done anything*?

The truth, which might have surprised Sasha, was that, of all the faculty and administration, the only one who had the balls to show up in the middle of the night was Josie. All the hypocrites and sweet-talkers, all those old men who crooned the words '*in loco parentis*' to us – well, none of them showed up. They slept soundly, waiting to die slow meaningless deaths in their warm beds.

I got the story from Raghav after he'd had his thigh wound cleaned and bound. After they left Surya, they had gotten into the car to go to the lake. On the way back, the treacherous old 800 ran out of gas. They tried to flag down a car to help. The Sumo they stopped was full of drunk men hungry for young women. They asked Sasha to cut them a deal. He told them to get lost. They got out and started pushing him around and, out of nowhere, a knife appeared. He had no chance. They stabbed him in the neck and the side and the upper arm and the chest, and he bled to death on the side of the road, choking on his own blood.

No one will ever be able to tell us what I want to know. What was it like for Sasha to stand there and see the shine of the knife, to know that there was no way out? Does your heart break when you know that there is no hope? In the rainy night, with the faces coming out of the dark, stranded in the middle of nowhere, what is the name for the courage it takes to stand up for those who cannot protect themselves?

I waited until dawn at the hospital. The morgue van came and took him away, wrapped up in a clean, white sheet. They had shut his eyes and mouth so he would look peaceful. I came back to the hostel in the early morning. Kelkar and Amlan were waiting at the door of the hostel. As I came up the path, they silently hugged me and made me go up and take a shower. I stripped on the way to the bathroom, throwing the jeans and shirt covered in Sasha's dried blood into the bin. When I came out, Kiran was waiting for me. We said nothing. We hugged and that was the end of it.

It was raining again the next day. I waited for the same van at the crematorium with Sasha's parents, Raghav in a white kurta, limping behind us. When they brought him in, we carried him to an old stone slab. In front of a mural of Hanuman kneeling, his father circled him as the priests chanted the prayers, holding a pot of ghee with a hole in it. No father should have to cremate his son. It violates the order of things; it leaves no one to light the last fire. The ghee poured down on Sasha like misfortune, soaking his winding sheet, spreading the rice on his chest. Then we hoisted him on our shoulders and carried him to the fire, my socks soaked in ghee and slipping on the stone floor. It was raining outside as the body slid into the iron oven and the door closed. From within came the smell of ghee on fire.

I went outside with everyone else, but something made me turn around and go back in. I walked to the oven and sat there, talking to the oven door, telling him things. The attendant came up behind me noiselessly and coughed to signal his presence. He asked if I wanted to look inside. I cannot tell you what animus made me say that I did, what hunger for certainty compelled me to say yes.

He cranked open the door and, each time I closed my eyes for the next week, what I saw there flashed before me like a negative. When all the fat and clothing and skin burns away, muscle fibres remain and tauten in the heat. Sasha was sitting up in the oven, one leg casually hanging to the side of the cement block, propping himself up on an elbow. A phantom of fire.

Today I am back there again, in that crematorium on Double Road, smelling flesh and ghee burn. Lying in bed, thousands of miles away, a year later, I turned the pages of my Tolkien to where the Nazgul surround the hobbits. In my bedroom, it's a dark night on Weathertop, as the hobbits climb the inner passages of the old watch hill to its ringed top. In the melee in the dark, the witch-king of Angmar stabs Frodo in the shoulder, and he carries that wound till it is healed by the elves of Rivendell. But, for every year after, in early October, the pain rises till it immobilizes Frodo and then passes away. Chapter XI of *The Fellowship of the Ring*. It's called 'A Knife in the Dark'.

gouge away

The Pixies/Doolittle/1989

After Sasha died, everything changed. It's as if someone had turned the lights on and opened the exit doors in the middle of a play. Well, go on, he had said, you can't stay here forever. Get a move on.

We all did. The run-up to recruitment and graduation would have been important and tense anyway, but, after that, it was as if all the colour had drained from the community. The Surya terrace was abandoned. People spent more and more time in the library or in their rooms. The quad was empty most of the time.

For my part, I caught the flight out after the cremation, went home and slept for two straight days and nights. When I woke up, there was nothing in my mind. It was quiet like the lake at night. Then it all came home, spiralling downward like a carrion bird out of the sky, striking to kill. I held my head in my hands and waited for tears. They never came.

I thought about not going back to Law School. But in the cold light of morning, the idea was ridiculous. When I came back, it was as an adult, with a job to look for and a quick six months to do what must be done and then turn my back on Bangalore forever.

I came back afraid of everything. I'd go out, but I'd carry a knife in my bag. I'd take only main roads and stick to crowds. Safety in numbers; nobody can pick you off in a group. The sight of unemployed young men would strike a chill down my spine. I'd turn and walk the other way, one hand on the flap of my bag.

I pussied out of things in worse ways than I had ever thought possible. If someone had said something to antagonize me, earlier, I might have tried to brazen it out. Now I just walked faster.

None of this was conscious. A truth had just registered in my head. The human body is a fragile sac of organs, blood and electrical impulses, which functions in a narrow range of climates and temperatures and stops functioning when pierced by a tiny slug of metal, or cut with a knife. Even blunt force trauma, like being hit by a car or a heavy object, can shake it so hard that it ceases to function, even if there is no rupture in the fragile membrane. Electric current can stop the heart. Water can enter the lungs and end the process of respiration. You could choke on a fishbone and that would be the end of it. Things can change in a second. Your luck could turn anytime.

They say that death is a part of life. That's untrue. We live in the midst of death. Death is no stranger. There are millions more dead than alive, millions of dead people, plants that are coal, beasts who are skeletons. There are once-living things everywhere on earth; in the ice and snow of the highest mountains, at the bottom of the oceans, in the thinnest, most unsubstantial airs of the atmosphere. Even where there is nothing, no air, no oxygen, no sunlight – around the undersea volcanoes spewing sulphur and nitrogen, there are bacteria which derive energy from that and fix it in mussels and shells. All of them cling to life as long as they can, as far as biology and effort can take them. But the angel of death comes for every living thing, his wings sweeping away thin air, sulphurous water, ice and snow equally.

Something had changed in the city. It was no longer the same place where we spent nights sleeping on the steps of cinemas, or you could hitch a ride with anyone. Some trigger point had been reached and we were clear outsiders, no longer welcome.

We turned inward. Kelkar pulled off a job with Goldfarb Remington in London and started researching the cuts of the suits he'd take with him. Amlan, Kiran, Raghav and I went into the waiting game, waiting for campus recruitment and the big Indian firms to come down and pick us up.

Seshadri filled out applications to foreign colleges and moaned on about statements of intent. He spent his spare time smoking pot with Rathore, the only man whose mind could understand him and stretch him. Now that the long distance race of building up a grade point average and publishing articles was run, he could afford to take it easy. At any rate, his name on a paper was enough to earn him at least an A+, whether he had put any work into it or not. He decided to take the last six months of college off.

Amlan turned so bitter that he was impossible to talk to; every conversation turned to the things going wrong in his life. He would dwell on his grades, look through the four years past, asking himself where things had gone wrong. He had fallen in love with the idea of his own depression. He sat in his room with the lights off and smoked endless packs of small bitter Gold Flakes and listened to the Sisters of Mercy.

Jennifer went into a worse depression, but wasn't as obvious about it. Her grades were as bad as Amlan's, only she didn't want the law firms that Amlan did. She wanted the company counsel jobs with the large household names, nurturing environments and decent work-life balances. But her insecurities about her lack of interest in the law and the prejudice that awaited her in the working world had sapped her confidence to the point where she would have broken down in an interview. She needed constant comforting, and I felt less and less interested in doing it.

Then I would wonder if maybe Kiran might have been there for her to a greater degree. Would he have sat her down and helped her with interview prep? Would he have helped her research the companies showing up and the kinds of law they cared about – intellectual property and product regulation? How long would he have been patient?

After Sasha died, Raghav went mute for weeks. He didn't speak to anyone about anything. He left campus every day after class and only came back in time for the next day's classes. Then, one day, he came to my room.

'Can I come in for a bit?'

'Sure,' I said, shocked. Why would Raghav even ask? Raghav, who for years had been walking into any room he wanted, borrowing whatever he needed and walking out without a word?

'I want to talk to you. About Sasha.'

'Go ahead. What are you thinking about, the trial?'

'No. Can I, ummm, shut the door?'

'Sure.'

Raghav sat down on my bed and drew his knees up. 'This is something I haven't told anyone.'

He paused and rummaged about, avoiding my gaze. I held my peace.

'That day, I didn't have any gas in my tank. So I came in here to borrow Sasha's car keys. I took it to the bakery and back.'

The whole snake of causality unwound before me. If Sasha had the extra kilometre worth of gas, he would have been able to get to Surya, walking distance from college. He would have walked it down and left the car outside Surya. The next morning, he or I or whoever needed the car the most would have gone to retrieve it with a Coke bottle full of petrol. He'd have cursed and delayed it and made it a chore. And Sasha would be alive.

In Raghav's head, he had killed Sasha as surely as if he had plunged that knife into his throat. He knew, of course, all the things I tried to tell him. That it was merely a happenstance, an unfortunate parallel fact, that Sasha would have made a dozen stupid pointless trips that day, skipping any of which would have saved his life, that there was no rational basis for his guilt. I tried to instil in him the faith that, if he did not act evilly, he could do no evil. To no avail; in his head Raghav believed he killed Sasha.

When he was leaving my room, I asked him where he was off to.

'To Kelkar's room. I think we need to talk.'

He smiled thinly and left.

calm like a bomb

Rage Against the Machine/ The Battle of Los Angeles /2000

I was woken up in the middle of the night by Kelkar calling from London. That's how I heard that Bombay was burning. They came by boat this time, streaking in to the bay on little black rafts, and attacked everything that had drawn us to the city. They shot up Leopold's, the Oberoi, the Taj on the bay and Colaba Causeway and the Gateway, bullets streaking through the muggy night. I can see them jumping off their rubber rafts at Gateway, where the ferries leave for Elephanta, and then running through the arch firing ahead of themselves. When I turned on the TV, the Taj was already on fire, the dome lit up from behind.

Bombay, where Sasha and I spent so many nights together as penniless interns, turning our pockets out for one of Leopold's gravity-assisted beer tubes. Where we sat at the Gateway and smoked hash with friendly Nigerians. The gas station where Sasha and Amlan bought cigarettes, lit them and got yelled at for nearly blowing up Colaba. The Causeway where you can buy sexy straw chappals and feel like half a hippie. That Bombay.

No work is happening at the office this morning. Everyone has the news running in a window on their screen. The reporters are doing their headless chicken act, substituting emotion for information. The talking heads have taken their seats in the boxes on the screen. Everywhere the old debate has broken out again. Are terrorism laws consistent with democracy? Can preventive detention ever be legal? Would the BJP have let this happen?

I'm scared of the way this country will go. I see a vicious right turn. There'll be a lot more insincere flag-waving, and a lot of ominous laws. More tikas, more tridents, more threats. And I don't trust the police. To me they'll always be the harsh voice to the outsider, a stick on the back, the barrel of a gun and the path of least resistance.

Sasha's killer got the treatment from the cops. When Seshadri and I went to the station, the guy was up on a wall, doing the time-honoured aeroplane, his arms tied to hooks. The bruises on his chest and thighs had deepened to an eggplant purple. His head was resting on the amulets on his chest and his hair covered his eyes. There was dried blood around his mouth. I cannot recall his face, only a thin boyish body hanging from a wall. I turned around and walked out of the station, down the steps, to where there was more air.

At four in the morning, when all your shawl-and-jholawallahs are asleep, sadistic red-eyed inspectors lean back in their chairs, flicking peanuts at the underwear-clad shadow on the wall. Never mind *D.K. Basu* or any of the judiciary's other limp-wristed fops towards human rights, never mind the constitutional right against self-incrimination; torture is the first tool of authority. When you're down there, it doesn't matter who you are or whom you know or where your rights lie – in the darkness, the only power in the world is the power exercised on your body. Across the country, in every station, in every holding cell, in the basement below every station, is a torture chamber. They've been doing it so long that they've made a science of it. No cuts, no permanent trauma, nothing that will stand up in court. So they beat the soles of your feet and run electrical charges through your groin and suspend you till the muscles in your shoulders and arms tear and break.

How does it matter who killed Sasha or what comes of the trial? I get emails every month about bail hearings, evidence hearings, the public prosecutors' submissions. Retributive justice grinds fine to punish the murderer; and yet, to me, nothing of consequence has taken place.

What would Sasha think? Maybe in the beginning, he would have been furious and angry, and firing on all cylinders. He might even have pushed for the death penalty. But in the course of time, I suspect, he would have come to some kind of forgiveness.

I don't know how we'll deal with all of the world's evil, the terrorists at Churchgate, the soldiers who rape women in the hinterlands, the criminals who murder students in the night. People say we need to find the right balance of procedural justice and state strength. That's easy to say. I think we need an age of saints.

The last time I met Sasha's parents, his mother told me with the tone of someone who expects to be doubted that she thought he had been a saint, sent down to earth to teach and help people, to infuse something holy and loving into them. His father cleared his throat so as to call humbug on it, but with no real sense of denigration. I yarred and yawed and dodged the proposition, because I also knew the kind of capricious bastard he was capable of being. How he could say one thing in one room and the exact opposite in the next room. But, in a strange way, none of his frailties took away from the truth about Sasha. In a way none of us were, he was *pure*. He was *pure* like sunlight, like clean snow, like the sap of plants. He was the least poisoned by the world, the least cut down and discouraged, the least compromised.

There's a story in it; something legendary in the way Sasha's life wound down. Born on a ship in the icy waters of a northern Russian port, floes floating in the water; named after an old port hand, who in turn was named after saints. Visions of his school in the hills, the grey wool blazers and green pines. Visions of him in the sun, walking around barefoot, giving his money to needy strangers. Reading the newspaper in his boxers on the terrace. Putting in a tackle and coming away with the ball, moving up the gears smoothly like a sports car. Eating hot, greasy rabbit kebabs on the footpath in Koramangala. The way he could never hide his emotion, his face crinkling in rage or laughter or derision, loving generously and carelessly, hating volubly and in passing.

On his first birthday after he died, on a cold December night, the sky pink and purple with reflected light, Amlan, Kelkar and I drank to him on the hostel terrace. We poured out a drink for him, a rum and coke, and the thirsty concrete drank it up. Then we got drunker than we should have, and I have only a hazy and jagged vision of Kelkar shouting against the bright night, his back bent like a bow. I don't remember what he was shouting about.

Somehow, we were all clear on one thing, that we were immeasurably richer for having known him. And if Sasha was the angel's share, then the angel took too much.

go your own way

Fleetwood Mac/Rumours/1976

Kiran was in Delhi last night. I met him at a dive bar – the sort of bar that starts life as a perfectly respectable establishment, with an attempt at decor, theme menus, a distinction between waiters and the maître d', and then becomes a piece of the economic problem that is liquor. At one of these, which was once a Mexican place, I met Kiran, Swati and Amlan.

The memory of the night I learnt about Swati and Kiran buoyed up like the slice I squeezed into the throat of my Corona. All these memories of the endgame are bitter like a lime. On that night in the winter of our fifth year, Jennifer called me sounding frantic and I went to see her at the library. She hugged me and started bawling. When I coaxed it out of her, she said, 'They've taken Brown Brown away.'

'Who's taken Brown Brown away?'

'The Municipality. They took all the strays.'

I was both shocked and relieved. This wasn't serious; did she really care that much for that weak-eyed perpetually drooling mutt? I reassured her, murmuring, 'They'll let them go in the woods. He'll come back, baby. They all do.'

'But,' she sniffed, 'he's so stupid. He'll get killed.'

I had no answer. That dog was literally retarded.

She dried her eyes and then a fresh flood began.

'Kiran called. He's seeing Swati.'

I felt a great weight of guilt lift off me. 'Aren't you happy?'

No. She wasn't. It wasn't enough for her that he was now free and happy. She hadn't even loved him that much, not the way she loved me. When she left him and came back to me, it broke him. Now he was whole again, but he was no longer hers.

She wanted more. I guess we all want more. At that moment, I now think, she must have felt like one of the Brown Browns of the world, who will never have the togetherness to get around well enough.

But she wasn't stupid, not like Brown Brown. I should have said so that night, but I didn't know that that was her secret fear. But more than that, she wasn't sure that I would be around next year.

Jennifer knew the truth. She knew that I loved her. But she also knew the whole truth.

'Some days,' she said, one night at Surya, 'some days, you actually love me.'

'I always love you.'

'No, not every single day. Some days you have to think about it. But some other days, you actually love me.'

I looked at the Old Monk bottles and the cola and the squeezed limes, with their cilia of squeezed pods. That day I did love her.

'No, I really do love you all the time. Sometimes I don't show it. That's how it is, no? You're the same.'

She looked at me carefully. 'No, I love you all the time. It's not your fault.' Then she smiled and hopped over into my lap.

Thankfully, at that very moment, Kelkar joined us. He was pissed off about the nuclear deal and we let his political concerns and the black rum take us away.

The second time around, the equations were different. There was the additional strain of the fact that both of us had made a decision to be there. She had left someone who loved her, who worshipped the ground she treaded on. I had turned my back on the infidel world of perpetual motion for her – and trodden on my friend. It would be a bit shit if this too frayed and broke, wouldn't it?

That history lay on the ground around us like the dark shadow of the next building. It made us tell half-truths and, sometimes, it made us lie. Like a tricky odometer, it misled us about how much gas we had in the tank. The truth was that we were running on empty for a long while before the engine gave out.

One morning, just before recruitment, Jennifer pulled me out of bed for her interview with Intel and we went across the city to the Intel campus, through broken-down east Bangalore and the brown dust that envelops the dejected suburbs, with their half-full housing developments. The roads were broken by the perpetual rain, which had left them covered with rubble and indistinguishable from the rubble. The sidewalk watermelon sellers wiped their carts down and sprinkled their goods to make them appear fresher than they were.

I was still half asleep when we got there, waking up intermittently to revise patent law and massage her neck.

But what I remember most clearly was Jennifer's reaction to the Intel campus. How, out of the brown dust, they had landscaped and watered a perfect green jewel, with neatly manicured grass, hedges exactly waist high, trees all the same height, shaped like the spades on a deck of cards. The way the inner roads were swept clean and painted bright, the third of each road marked 'Walk here' and it all fitted in, with the intelligent ID cards and the fast food outlets, the gift shop, the crèche, the metal detectors, the little fountain, the housing developments across the street. They had created a Legoland, and locked out all the chaos and anarchy of the world outside. Jennifer clutched my arm delightedly. It felt so perfect to her, so accepting, so safe and comforting; the prospect of knowing exactly how long her work day would be, of rising slowly and steadily in the echelons of the megacorporation, of steadily larger offices, from the cubicle to the cabin and then, at the same time as a child and family and the purchase of a house, the corner office.

In contrast, I felt unease and, worse, a deep-seated contempt for her aspirations. The idea of playing football with the Intel team, for the honours in corporate tournaments, where everyone gets a prize. The idea of watching Jennifer covering soft rock songs with the Intel band, an eternity of 'Don't Stop Believing'. I could never bring myself to walk between two yellow lines. I love too much the anarchy and dust of cities, of music and strangers and the uncertainty of new food and new places.

Maybe that was the difference between us in the end. That Jennifer had grown up and wanted these things: stability, sanity, certainty. She wanted to know she would go to her home that night and live in comfort, and that her world could be neat, clean and happy; progressive and free from incident.

Some of us are meant to settle down, put down roots, pick up tools and make loan payments. Some of us are meant to keep walking.

She might not have known the truth of it, but she was right when she said I had taken the best years of her life. I laughed it off. Even she laughed off the corniness of the statement. She meant the years she looked slimmest and most beautiful. But what I shared with her in that time we were together was that one crystalline spark of adventure she was given, and her native genius striving to be free. I saw her beautiful in the morning in strange places, and later I saw her struggling with and losing her footing in the world. So, yes, I guess did take the best years of her life, but she didn't even know it.

The second time around, there was so much silence. Silence as a substance, like mounds of sugar in a refinery, silence you could drown in, an inviolable silence. Silence like a wall, under the bright yellow lights of the footpath.

'I thought,' she says with the sob pronounced, 'I really thought we'd make it to the end together.'

I feel time pile up on me, the years together, every day of watching her eyes. And I see how close that finish line was. Couldn't I have hung on just a little longer? But I have nothing to say. I have no lines in this scene. So I say nothing. Above our heads, insects swirl in interlocking inexact helices, turning and swirling their thousands of lives above us.

I fight my inertia, trying to say something. I feel a sickness in my bowels, so deep, so deep. 'I tried as long as I could.'

It is the truth and she laughs with infinite bitterness to hear it. 'But you can't wait, na? It was so hard for you to be with me.' Silence. Laugh. 'Then go.'

The word 'go' is gentle. It is an unwrapping of cotton, a loosening of bonds, an ebbing of water.

I say nothing. She stands up to go, rewrapping her shawl. She starts, then she stops. 'But … just hug me once.'

I hold her and I feel her heart beating through the fabric. She clings one last time, like she is trying to leach the last flavour from something. I feel dizzy, sickened by my countering urges. To walk away and start over, or to hold in my arm this weak beast to whom I owe so much. So it is I who pry her away gently. She looks at me with accusation in her eyes and then she walks away.

I wanted to tell her then, but I was mute. I wanted to tell her that I was powerless to turn things around. The teabag has been squeezed till it holds nothing more. Plants and animals come to an end. Seasons turn. The wind changes direction. Eyes open. They close. Songs end. The sun rises. When something is finally over, when it is too thin, spread out too far, it will snap.

Watching her walk down the path, I was the saddest winner in the world, free of my burden finally. She walked into the darkness, angry and bitter, carrying the still burning cinder of our time together. She took it away and, since then, I have been near no fire hot enough to burn.

the shape of things to come

Audioslave/Revelations/2006

In fifth year, you're a different kind of student, capable, mature. The research papers that used to torture you for weeks in first year are now the work of a long night or two. The law isn't merely a language that you can speak, it's a world you inhabit, the way a fish swims through water. It only takes a glance at a judgment or a page of a textbook to place a concept within the arcology of the legal world. The subjects you study become more advanced and specialized – banking, intellectual property, environmental law.

The same ease applies to the world of Law School. No idiosyncrasy of the institution or its inhabitants shocks or dismays any longer. You know the rules, the risks, the strategies. But, at its darkest, the night covers everything. Nothing is unsullied. Even when the dawn has started breaking, the light must resist the tendrils of dark slipping into it, bleeding it.

Through all the trouble we had put ourselves in, Seshadri had kept his academic nose clean. He had topped the class by a very decent margin. He had bagged half a dozen gold medals in the process. As befits a man of his stature, Seshadri had gotten through to the interview stages for the Rhodes scholarship. Every year since 1995, the Rhodes committee ended up selecting one lawschoolite for the scholarship. In Seshadri's case, it was a foregone conclusion. His credentials, his extra curriculars, his ability to project the best of himself, they all pointed the way to Oxford Union. No one grudged him this; every other Law School candidate was only hoping the committee loved him or her enough to sanction one college a second spot.

Seshadri took the weekend off to go to Hampi. He went with his new friends, the only people who weren't busy shitting themselves over jobs. Ever since Sasha's death, he had spent increasingly more time with Rathore and Faiza. Something escapist and bohemian in his makeup was tickled by their pursuit of absolution in chemical realms, by their Sid and Nancy act. To properly relax himself for the interview stages, he had decided to take a little drug holiday with them in a suitably majestic location. Rathore, who viewed his time with Seshadri as a kind of tuition, decided this was the weekend Seshadri would drop acid for the first time.

Rathore, Faiza and Seshadri put up at a little lodge frequented by groups of backpackers. It was the kind of lodge where the management had no choice but to disclaim every activity that went on. Which is why, when the police came looking for Seshadri's room, they were happily shown to a room where Rathore and Faiza lay unconscious, entwined and naked on the bathroom floor. Seshadri had left the room jabbering and raving, and the door was wide open.

They picked up Seshadri under a streetlight on the corner. The white bed sheet that was all he wore had slipped down to his waist. He had placed a watermelon on the power box under the streetlight and was worshipping it, his brown back bent over the paving stones. The facts lend themselves to some perverse theory of atavistic predetermination, don't they? Seshadri's ancestors had been priests since the beginning of recorded history. In whatever world he entered, in whatever state, worship was to have been his mode of action.

He spent the night in jail and, when his folks showed up, he was almost sober. Luckily, the cops could find no drugs on him or in the room. They released him to his parents with a lecture and a shakedown.

At the Rhodes interview the next day, his hands shook. By all accounts, he was calm and composed, and his suit was immaculate; nothing less than what you'd expect from Seshadri. But it didn't matter. Someone had informed the Rhodes committee that the person before them had spent a night in jail for public disturbance. No one has any secrets before the committee; the level of competition is far too high, and the selection criteria too unforgiving.

So Seshadri broke the streak. It was the first time in ten years that NLS had not fielded a Rhodes scholar. There might only be a couple of hundred people on the planet who would look on not winning the Rhodes as a miserable failure, and Seshadri was one. Every job, every other scholarship to every other university in the world, was his for the asking; but the one thing he wanted above all, he could never have.

Amlan and I spent our last month in college together sitting on the terrace as he smoked. We spoke of many things, jobs, money, cars, audio equipment, music. The most important things were always left unsaid, because Amlan disdained the intangible and, in the atmosphere of his disdain, I was uncomfortable.

In that last stretch of college life, our eyes were always on the prize, regardless of whose prize it seemed to be. The glitz of the quick-moving world, the climbing Sensex, the sudden introduction of sense into Bollywood flicks, the Kingfisher calendar, the sheen of New India calling to us.

We were listening to Audioslave, a step away from the ideological roots of Rage Against the Machine and the black denial of Soundgarden. Audioslave were somehow *credible* without being great.

The best way to explain the style of Audioslave is a scene in an absolutely crap movie, *Miami Vice*, a Colin Farrell and Jamie Foxx flick without any of the camp cheesiness that redeemed the show. Colin Farrell approaches the suitably mysterious oriental lady protagonist and she asks him what he likes to drink. He says he likes mojitos. She says she'll take him to a place with great mojitos. Cut. Next scene, they're speeding across the water in a boat so fast it barely touches the waves, to Havana, for mojitos. At night, after some vigorous salsa dancing, the moon shines down on the beach, the characters start making out and the camera goes into soft focus as Audioslave's 'Shape of Things to Come' plays. That's pretty much the epitome of glamour to two guys sitting on a rooftop in Nagarbhavi.

This was the world revealed to us in the same breath as the leveraged buy-out – Tata's acquisition of Corus, Mittal storming Arcelor – and a growing realization of our adult potential. Naturally, our conception of glamour was hard-bitten and rough around the edges. Amlan had worked very hard for his smoker's throat.

'So, if everything goes well, then what? You get TSMS and then you work hard for ten years. Then you become a partner and when you finally have enough money, you're old. What'll you do with it then?'

'I don't want to be a lawyer very long. I just want the money for a few years, and then I want to do something else …'

'What?'

'I don't know. I want to do something different. I want to write for *Rolling Stone*.'

He emits a short laugh, like a bark. Then he gleefully unwinds my plan. 'See, it will take you five years to earn any real money, because for the first two years, you'll only spend, because you'll want a car and a home theatre and you'll want to go clubbing and do lots of fine dining and shit to make up for all these years of penury. Then by the time you earn any real money you'll be almost thirty, and you will be required to get married and have kids. Once you have kids, you have to stick with being a lawyer, because you need the income and nothing else pays so well. If you want to become a banker, which is the only other thing you can become when you have a family, you have to stop earning for two years to do an MBA and then you have to work really hard to make up for lost time. So, by the time you're finally important enough to matter, you'll be fifty, and after that, it's time to die anyway.'

Triumphantly he lights a cigarette, snapping his metal lighter shut. I gag at the thought of this long downward slide to the grave.

I make a blustering comeback. 'What about you?'

'I'm going to become a private equity specialist. Then I'll join a private equity firm like Blackstone and then I'll keep making lateral shifts until I become head company counsel for some big Indian company.'

'Hey! That'll also take you about fifteen years.'

Again, the laugh. 'Yeah. We're all fucked.'

'You're just being an asshole because your boyfriend is out of town.'

Around Nicki, everything was different. Amlan was so fiercely possessive of Nicki that he did not speak of him to anyone. It was a sight for the faithless, watching them walk together – Amlan holding Nicki like a miser holds a jewel, Amlan's strong, callous attitude and Nicki's diffidence. Around him, Amlan's blackness dissolved and drained away. He never even said much, just smiled blissfully and you knew he had found the only pursuit in which his joy would not fade. I imagined that, in private, he confessed all his happy thoughts, his hopes and dreams to Nicki, so that he could distil the poisonous cynicism into an extra strong decoction for his friends.

The half of whisky came to an end. This was the worst possible thing to happen. We'd only had about a quart each and so neither of us were even meaningfully high. It was already midnight, so the guards wouldn't let us out to get more booze, besides which, it would have meant a twenty-kilometre trip to Rosie Bar in town. At that point, two first years came up to the terrace with a friendly-looking black bag. Prey, it appears, and Amlan is hungry.

'What's your name, cutie?'

'My name is Anil Saxena, sir.'

'Great. Very proud of you. Don't you want to know what my name is, Anil?'

'May I please know your name, sir?'

'You don't need to call me sir, honey. We're a community of equals here. My name's Amlan.'

'Thank you, Amlan.'

'As an equal, I request ... No, I insist, that you touch my testicles.'

'No!'

'Why won't you touch my balls? Is it because I'm queer? You think I'll enjoy it?'

'No. Of course not.'

'Who're you kidding? Right, so you'd cup Zorawar's sack? It's a mark of respect around here.'

'That's right. Cup my sack.' There's no such thing as ragging without a wingman.

'I don't want to touch anyone's balls.'

'How does it matter what you want? If I want you to cup my bullahs, you better cup them like they're precious pearls. Get to it.'

I felt the need to lend persuasion. 'If you don't touch his balls, and it gets out that you didn't listen to a fifth year, no senior will ever help you do research or anything. In fact, I think we might have a word with the student disciplinary committee. You know what they can make you do, right? Are you a morning person?'

'I guess.'

'Well, you won't be guessing when you have to wake up at five-thirty to count milk packets in the mess. So, son, I suggest you cradle Amlan's tattas.'

The first year, on the verge of tears, steeled himself, closed his eyes and grabbed Amlan's crotch. Amlan let out a shriek and the first year jumped back confused. I went spastic with laughter.

'You touched my balls, you pervy bastard! I'm going to fucking kill you! I'm going to rip out your eyeballs and skullfuck you!'

Now, Amlan has it as bad as I do. Nicki moved abroad and, over time, everything fell apart. Amlan's put the weight back on and he smokes two packs a day. When he gets off work at four in the morning, he drives across the Bandra-Worli Sea Link at 150 kilometres an hour in his Zen with the dodgy suspension and the windows open. If he hit a pebble at that speed, that car would flip and he would disappear into the Arabian Sea and leave no traces. If he wrenched the wheel sideways, that possibility would become a certainty. He does it because he doesn't care whether he lives or dies anymore, because he's trapped and he can't see a way out, and the way forward is too dismal. He's out of luck and out of love and plumb out of ideas.

We are told a lie at birth; the lie no parent can avoid telling. We are told that we are special, that we are a unique imprint on reality, that we can do anything we want to, be anything we want to be. We are all told this from the day we're born, and we are old in the world before we realize that it cannot possibly be true. By that time, it is no longer an idea that can be denied or a hope that can be dashed. It is an ingrained standard we can never measure up to; an ache we can only soothe, never root out entirely.

It is the reason we are unhappy with compromises, unhappy to sit in the order of things, unhappy to take the slow way up. Which is what our parents did, and they don't hesitate to tell us about their struggles. But that is not our vision. Our visions are based on the original lie, and all the beautiful lies we are told by storybooks and fairytales and cinema, by those cunning old bastards, Jules Verne and Alexandre Dumas and Cecil DeMille, and all the ancillary and accessory shopkeepers and columnists and friendly uncles who are equally culpable for poisoning our heads with fiction. Somewhere, we were promised more: the key to the secret garden, the philosopher's stone, the moons of Saturn. Until we conclusively find out that it doesn't exist, we remain adolescents, forever waiting to become something.

When recruitment time came around, all of us sat in the interview centre in shirts and ties, waiting for interviews, waiting for others to make their choices. Looking at each other, knowing that in the next forty-eight hours, everything would sort itself out. Inside everyone's head, the insecurity built up like water pressure. I wished that I could trade everything, all the fun, all the trips and all the tripping for higher grades. Amlan wished he had anything at all on his CV, that he hadn't scorned everyone's activities.

Worst of all, Jennifer was in the bathroom, wishing that she wasn't from the Northeast, trying to wash away her identity, knowing that it would lower her chances of being hired. That was day one of recruitment. On day two, she disappeared.

They say it's impossible to disappear in the modern world. You would have left internet traces or a credit card trail.

Your family and friends would always know. Unless you're Jason Bourne, somebody would always be able to point even the most casual seeker in your direction.

Bullshit. This is how you could disappear completely:

1) Find a large city. And no city in India is larger and more inscrutable than Delhi.
2) Find an ethnic ghetto of Delhi, a low-rent, low-income area, where no one asks too many questions and nobody answers any.
3) Find a boyfriend nobody from your past life knows. His friends will be your friends. His bank account will be your bank account.
4) Transact only in cash. You don't actually need plastic for anything.
5) Don't drive and nobody will ever ask you for ID for anything.
6) Get a new prepaid mobile phone connection with a random address. This step is optional.
7) Just stop using the internet. Orphan your Gmail and Facebook and Orkut accounts. They'll wait for you, if you ever want them again.

You're done. Now you're invisible. Never go to the parts of Delhi where people from your past life might go, which are surprisingly few, and you may never be spotted. In a few years, you can be so forgotten that no one would care anyway.

At least, that's how I guess Jenni did it.

But I'm still not clear why. Two months from finishing college, two months from being a lawyer, she upped and left. No one even noticed; when I asked around, no one could point to the day. She had retreated so far from people and snapped at so many people that, when she shut her door, nobody knocked, and then she just decided to call it. She didn't pack much. She took a suitcase and a bag and left.

I barely noticed. We had stopped talking a long time ago, made sure we shared no classes, and she had disappeared from public life. I was busy making the most of my last few months of college, and I checked into and checked out of reality more often than I should have. Finally, by the time I felt her absence, she was gone into the city like a snail into a dark pond.

There are hundreds of thousands of young people without college degrees working nights in call centres and earning enough to pay rent, working in offices as help staff, making coffee and writing screenplays. They exist as a demographic – corporate lawyers and investment bankers don't. These young people influence tastes and markets. They're the people watching movies in the day and listening to the radio and eating potato chips. They make the giant greasy dusty machine of our country work. This is young urban India – it asks very few questions and it's always hungry. From the outside, it's impossible to look in.

bullet with butterfly wings

The Smashing Pumpkins/Mellon Collie and the Infinite Sadness/1995

The first sign that things were going to get strange was when Jennifer's friend Evelyn called me one day on my way to work. She told me she had heard from Jen. I felt the way you do when, quite out of context, someone mentions a person close to you, a queasy sense of curved mirrors.

'Zoju, first you've got to promise me that you won't go looking for her.'

I suddenly felt sapped of all energy, a bone-deep sadness. Why does this stuff keep coming back to me?

'OK. Just don't give me her number.'

Evelyn told me many things. She said Jen was tired and she didn't sound like herself. Jen had told her she had been in and out of hospitals. I stopped my car by the side of the road, watching flyover traffic whiz past, wondering what it was; was it her blood pressure, was it a pill overdose? Had she slit her wrists again?

Then she told me many other things. She told me Jen was engaged to marry. She told me that Jen now smoked Gold Flakes, didn't drink because he didn't drink, because a single beer would get him drunk. Evelyn sounded vindictive today. She told me it had been a small victory for her to get Jen to have a beer the last time she saw her.

I wonder, what does poor sad Evelyn see in me that she would throw me this nugget? Why, after I destroyed Jennifer's life, does she feel like I deserve to know anything? The visions in my head have a self-contained cinematic quality. Somewhere, Jen and her fiancée could be standing on a balcony drinking tea out of mismatched mugs, their hips touching. Or perhaps she has risen late, and he's lying in bed possessively watching her move around. Maybe they're both still in bed. Suddenly it strikes me that, while I'm stuck playing the same games I have been for years, chasing girls I don't know, maybe she's the one who's moved on, who's following up on some of the big adventures that adulthood grants you a right to participate in.

Maybe her mother taught her well, taught her to spin the mystery that occupies a man like a cat unravelling yarn. It is beyond me to guess the source of the warmth of her smile; to understand why the fact that she walked like a boy, with the bounce of a street urchin, used to fill me with a warm rush. But I do know that no one compares to her.

Somehow, I want Jennifer to know this: I have had no lovers like her. None so sapient, nor so luminous. I have had taller and thinner and tauter, but none so engrossing and wine-like, none whose notes of pettiness and bitterness warmed my heart as hers did. Every flavour I have encountered since has been thinner and poorer.

Little by little, I have eroded my ties to the past. My lovers are lost, perhaps irretrievably. My friends are far and occasionally met. Even in the mirror, I sense myself moving away from what I used to be – even physically. Fat obscures the cheekbones. The nose has thickened. And worse than anything else, the eyes look dead, like fish on slabs of ice. They are not even the eyes of excess and delusion; they are simply some other person's eyes.

There's this sense of packing up about everything, a placing in boxes, relabelling and eroding away of thoughts and feelings. The things I touch and know are all moving, sailing away, leaving this gaping distance in between.

It's four in the morning now. But, in New York, it's early evening, and the bankers are waiting for us to get the document out to them. Dhruv came by again and left me yet another section to back up. So I follow everything on the drafted section with a pencil and check any factual statement against the agreements we've seen, the certificates of quality, the hundreds of approvals from government bodies. Line by line I go, the pettiest clerk in the world, hunched over this desk and keyboard, making sure everything tallies. This really is the most tangential application of legal knowledge.

There're only two other people in the office and I can see their desks lit up from above across the floor. At moments like this, I'm glad Sasha doesn't know what I do for a living. His contempt would cut like a knife.

My eyes are gritty with sleep and I can feel weakness in my arms and back, a dull throbbing. It's been two weeks of this now. Sleep rises and fades now as a desire. I've postponed it mentally, told it to go away till I can afford it. This will all be over in three more nights. I can take it – I know this as certainly as I know that there will be a time when I won't be able to take it anymore.

When I leave the office at dawn, the world is waking. Birds come to life, trees take their colour back from the night, morning joggers fill the parks with their unique old-person gaits. I hunch over the wheel and drive back to my flat carefully, because I am afraid I'll pass out if I stop focusing. I get home, fall into bed and shut my eyes. In New York, it is lunchtime; somebody at an investment bank on the other side of the world is biting into a sandwich. Hang them all, I think bleakly, hang them by their Hermes ties. Let the laces of their Ferragamo shoes dangle in the wind.

When you wake up after two hours of sleep, it is like rising from a tomb. The mind trails the body for seconds; there is no *a priori* sense to guide the waking body and the open eyes, no go-between to introduce you to the world. Then the immense wave of dull ache crashes over you, like a wave long coming. No coherent thoughts form, all is sensation and numbness. Now only grit will take you to your bathroom, a suicidal bloody-mindedness. Focus on the mirror, on the grime that has accumulated at the base of the tap. Try not to slit your throat while shaving unevenly.

All the while, you're thinking, like a Radiohead song, this is not happening. This is not my life. This is a dream, an illusion, a carefully set up forgery. This is not my face, not my hands; none of this is mine. This is not what I thought would happen when I was a child and I planned to grow up. I am still that child, and none of this has happened. This is a dream, and I will awake and commence my life, knowing the paths to avoid.

But this is no dream, it is a long and continuing tale of sodomy and the lash. Reality is branded across it by your aching back, the roughness of your tongue, the coughing fit you suffer as you brush your teeth. Wake up. Get dressed. Get to work.

Now, do it again. Do it tomorrow. Do it till March. Do it till closing. Do it till the sun comes so close to scorching the planet that all the seas boil and turn to vapour.

I feel like there's a scream building up deep within me, knocking on the roof of my mouth to be let out. It happens every time some partner wants to give me comments or attend a con-call. No thanks, I'd rather not, I feel like saying. I want nothing of you. I do not want your sweets. I don't want to do anything you do. I hate your softness and your slowness and deliberation and your dependency. I hate your attention to detail and your consistency. I hate tracking comments to other comments. I detest the way you can't even use keyboard shortcuts.

I may not be brave, but sometimes I am angry. I feel it every day. This isn't even righteous anger. It's a wave of little things: traffic, fatigue, irritation, boredom, insecurity, fear – all distilled into a mercury thermometer of rage which boils past safety in my head. I feel like screaming at people.

At lunch, we sit around cafeteria tables and eat our food. There's this female partner who likes to read out the movie gossip and talk about restaurant reviews. And every time she says something, some wanker like Dhruv, or some other GMPT or an apprentice GMPT supplements what she's saying, and if he can't supplement it, he rephrases. Even now, as we chew, the hierarchy is flexing and pulsing about us. Every year, smart, ambitious young people check into the programme and burn themselves up trying to make senior associate. Senior associates crawl over glass to make partner. Partners walk through fire to make equity partner. Equity partners elbow and jostle to be close to name partners. All of us seeking the same thing – the nutritious pap, the lucre that leaks from the teats of Messrs Lawrence and Kamraj. Everyone has only the pride that their station allows. And if King Lawrence calls, then all of us come as equal servants, scraping as we bow, as we approach the throne and kiss the ring.

All this while, under this poker face, I'm shouting obscenities like a Tourette's sufferer, like a monkey tossing turds.

I realize that there are many things that I don't care for, you bourgeois bitches. I don't care for your concerns and I don't care for your ambitions. I don't like talking about people who are becoming partners elsewhere. I don't like the way you talk about travel destinations and the resorts there as if they were equivalents. Shopping is not a sport. Movies are not a night out. Not while you're still alive.

Even your crimes are so small. Taking a bigger cut to issue a favourable opinion. Cheating on your wife with an associate on the make. Filing an even smaller income tax return than you did last year. No one cares, no one's watching. No one gives a damn that Dhruv is fucking one of the interns. No one cares that people hook up at the annual retreat. If even your sins are sins of cupidity and gormlessness, then what price your dreams and what price your ambition?

Somehow this inadequacy in your souls burns me. It makes me angry. I feel angry like a giant in bonds. Your pathetic and small desires make me feel scorn for you, and worse, scorn for myself that I live my life with people like you. Is this all you are – a catalogue of consumer desires? An endless list of acquisitions? And am I becoming like you?

I can feel my anger pound cool and crystallize in your ears, while you smile and nod. No, I'm not a foodie. What the fuck is a foodie? I like good food. But I'm not mesmerized by these kebabs. I know a hole in the wall in every part of this city where you can find kebabs made better than this, and served with more heat and spice and desire. I like sweating when I eat. I like washing my hands at a tap. I enjoy walking around in crowds. The world outside is petty and poor and dirty, steeped in blood and semen and sputum. But it is *beautiful*.

In fact, I don't share any of your desires. I don't get turned on by gadgets. I don't get turned on by cars. I need these things to do what they're made for, making calls and covering miles. I want to show you how empty all these toys of yours are. What'll it take? Maybe I should kidnap one of your spoilt kids, take the brat somewhere and send you a finger in the mail every fortnight till you repent, till you understand what respect for life is.

What does turn me on, you omit to ask?

The open road turns me on. Turning around on trails and looking back and seeing how far I've come. Green football fields in the sunlight, the smell of cut grass, a ball in flight. Books and music turn me on, when people are paying attention to them. A glint in the eye. Yellow light and mattresses on the floor. Laughter free from calculation. Waking up in new and strange places. Not knowing what may happen when I step aboard. Letting a car in the night take me away.

I remember sitting in that car once with Sasha, on one of our trips to town. He was driving, I was smoking.

'Tell me, Sasha, what do you dream about?'

He looked at me straight, and sometimes I wonder if this is memory or some phantasm I have engineered.

'I dream about journeys. What else does anyone dream of?'

perfect circle

R.E.M./Murmur/1983

She came back last night, out of the blue, with the force of a kick to the abdomen. A message on my phone that turned my blood to ice, sluggishly drifting through my system. Everything falls apart slowly, a watch exploding. Suddenly I know what regret and dread and fear are again.

I picked her up where her message said she would be, in the galactic arms of Connaught Place. She opened the door, got in and stared straight ahead.

'Hi.'

'Hi.'

What a pair of elegant bookends. What a nullification of conversation.

The old silence engulfs us. I have so much to say. Where do I start? How could I tell her I've wondered where she's been all these years? That I'm sorry?

'I'm sorry.'

She turns, genuinely puzzled, and I remember what her eyes look like. 'What? What are you sorry for?'

'Everything. All the things that happened with us.'

'Oh that. That's okay. I've forgotten all about that. I've had ... bigger things to deal with of late. Can we go somewhere where we can talk?'

I'm stunned. All the things I've been rerunning in my head, all the pasts I've been living, the monumentality of my sins – she's forgotten?

I think of all the places we could talk. I don't want to go to a bar, because we won't be able to hear each other. At a coffee shop, we'd be suffocated by the assumptions of everyone inside that we were seeing each other, or fighting with each other, or going to be something, or were friends. Where do you go when you need to talk to long-lost lovers who may hate you, but need to see you for some reason you can't comprehend?

So I drove to the Lodhi Gardens and parked outside. Although it's shut after eight in the evening, there's no way to lock it and we walk through the stiles into a forest of darkness. There are lights in the distance and our feet feel out the path. I'm suddenly taken back to all the times we've walked together in the dark, in cities, in forests. She walks next to me and I reach down for her hand, instinctively. The back of my hand hits the back of her hand. She pulls away. So much for forgetting.

When you walk through the last of the bushes, the world opens up before you. Free from the humbling imposed by hundreds of scrambling children and itinerant cricketers, the tombs are ethereal and immense, the stone glowing warm in the glowing yellow lights. We settle in one of the arches supporting the platform of the biggest tomb. Now we can talk.

She lights a fag and inhales gratefully. I watch her carefully, studying this creature and her habits, the evolution of her.

'You didn't smoke before.'

'Last couple of months. Zoju, I have leukaemia. If I live to worry about lung cancer, I'll be happy.'

Silence.

'They can cure that, right? They can fix it?'

'The medicines haven't been working. I'm starting chemotherapy next week.'

'That has to work, right?'

'It might. It might not. There's a chance it might not and then they have a last shot with bone marrow replacement.' She laughs, and it is a laugh bitter like the grinding of teeth.

'All of my hair is going to fall out, Zoju, and I wanted to see you while I still had hair.'

'You have beautiful hair, Jenni.' The words can't find their way out. My throat is suddenly full of blood vessels and nerves and spine and other things and there is no air to convert into words. 'You've always had beautiful hair.'

She looks at me and I realize she just can't dig why I'm complimenting her. I mean, am I going to try to sleep with her?

'Thanks Zoju. You have beautiful hair too. It's one of the things I liked about you. How've you been?'

Suddenly, and I know how inappropriate all of this is, after what she's told me, I start talking. I can hear myself in my inner ear, and I can hear how childish and small my problems are, how voluntarily induced. I hear myself bitching about work and hours and how I don't have anything else in my life, and I realize that I could fix all of these problems. But she can't fix her problems; her body's killing her and she's fighting it with everything she's got. And still I keep talking, because I need to talk and I don't know what to say that actually matters. I go on and on like a little wind-up toy. All my life, I've felt like I'm the one sentient being trying to tune into a mechanical universe. Tonight there's no doubt in my mind that I'm just another part of a stupid and random world.

Jennifer hasn't changed much. She looks the same, she walks the same, dresses the same, her hair is still beautiful, but her eyes have changed. They were once soft like the underdown of a pigeon and now they are hard, and there's an edge to her laughter. I, on the other hand, am fatter by ten kilos, am losing hair by the ounce, haven't slept in weeks, haven't been outdoors in months, dressed unthinkingly in a dour grey suit. The gradient of superiority has been inverted. I always thought I wanted more noble things than she did, and now, nothing could be further from the truth.

'So, Zoju, how's the love life?'

'I don't have the time for one,' I blustered, 'I'm too busy for love.' I hear myself and am horrified. That's the kind of thing Dhruv would say. I wish I could take back the words, make up some girl, make up a story to tell her.

She looks at me, excavates my loneliness and then says, 'Well, I may be on my death bed, but at least I'm still getting some.'

How arch. How true. For a moment I am swept by a kind of desperation, a sudden crumbling feeling and all I want to do is reach out for her, ask her if she'll have me back, tell her it was all just another big mistake, tell her it can all be okay, that I'm done spreading my seed around, that I'll give myself to her, in sickness or in health, in life or in death, hair or no hair, cancer or no cancer. But I can't. She's a proud golden bird in the yellow light, and she's so far out of my reach that it makes me want to cry.

In this stone world, again, I can sense the weight of things. I can feel the surrounding hand of death, the gravity of all the stone, the impending sense of the earth. I remember once sitting not far from here, with Sasha, and he was explaining to me what it was to be *great*. Maybe by the end of the year, the earth will claim Jennifer, the way it has claimed Ibrahim Lodhi and the way the river and seas have claimed Sasha. How can you be great with the angel of death watching you, the shadow of his wings eclipsing your soul, the air thin in his wake?

I drive Jennifer back. After what I have heard, I am amazed we can still make small talk. She asks me to drop her off at a crossing. I offer to drop her to where she's staying, but she declines. I turn to her, and this time, I want to hug her and hold her close, this broken toy, who has held me and harboured me, to whom I owe so much. What I get instead is the hug you get from a stranger, a sort of shoulder to the chest and quick release. I watch her walk away, and half of me wants to follow her into the mazes she has built for herself. But I don't. I watch her pass safely into memory and distance. Let her go. Let her live or die. This ended a long time ago and nothing remains anymore.

there's a light that never goes out

The Smiths/The Queen Is Dead/1986

Tonight Barcelona put Manchester United to bed in Rome. 2-0. The score line flatters United. Andrés Iniesta, Xavi Hernández and Lionel Messi just never let go of the ball. They played it back and forth like yarn between a weaver's fingers, touching it once and moving in a hidden pattern. For the United midfield, it was like being let into a hall of mirrors, or the reversible meaning of a pack of tarot cards. They chased, they faltered and then, most thrillingly, they surrendered. Ronaldo sulked, Rooney beat his chest like the beast he is and the wave rolled on. Alex Ferguson's juggernaut stopped at the gates. It will go no further. Ronaldo will go to Madrid over the summer. The moment is sealed with Lionel Messi kissing his shoe at the Stadio Olympico.

I raise a glass in a bar on the other side of the world.

Everything will be all right. Beautiful flowing football won the Champion's League. Pep Guardiola in his silk-lined jacket won the treble in his first year as coach. And I know that one day, those kids at Arsenal will be this good. They will be that little bit harder, more secure and confident than they are. Maybe next year, maybe the year after. But the truth is out – when beauty has strength, it can reshape the world in its image. Maybe it won't be Arsenal. But teams playing football the right way will win. There are still beautiful things in the world. I know this now. The feeling steals over me like a fever, an empowering secret. You have to keep faith. Some years you lose, and some years you win. But what you can't do is play nine men behind the ball all your life and not be found out, because when you lose, you won't be able to look at yourself in the mirror.

That's the question, isn't it? I can hear Sasha asking it. Who are you when you turn off the lights? If they took everything from you today – your bank account vanished, your job disappeared, your lease expired and your car was repossessed – what would you be? You can always lose. You could die tonight, of a heart attack or botulism or a knife in the throat. You could die of a bus falling on you. When the hand of the angel comes for you, you must take it, you cannot refuse him. But, if you died tonight, would you be happy with who you were? If you survive tonight, if the angel does not come for you, shouldn't you prepare for tomorrow night?

Suddenly, I'm no longer in this shiny bar with all of these people and the waiters carrying trays of margaritas. I'm back in the common room with Sasha, our feet up on a chair as we watched a mid-season game four years ago, and argued about whether it was more important for a team to have Vieras or Bergkamps. I can see Sasha leaning forward in anguish because I couldn't understand why it was important to play beautiful football. There's tension in the phalanges between his fingers, a vein throbbing in his temple. Sasha, who most believed in living beautifully.

Look at us all on the map. Start far out west in America. Seshadri at Yale, learning that it's okay to just be one of the best and not always the first amongst the best, learning to deal with the first real winter he's seen, watching the snow come down on the spires of buildings full of books and learning. He is free to frolic with knowledge and ideas and share them with others, and you can't call that poor. The world will still be his, and now maybe he'll value it.

Moving east, Kelkar is in London, and every morning he does 200 push-ups and half an hour on the stepper and then he puts on his suit and his long wool coat and goes to the City on the Tube. There he cuts and pastes and redrafts and refines documents that create derivative securities and take their value from bets and arbitrage and options. At night, when he goes somewhere to watch a play or hear some exciting new Ethiopian folk artist, he feels lost because he works very hard, but this is not his game, and he doesn't want to make it to the goal that lies at the end of it. Every night, he walks all the way home because he wants to let out all the puzzlement and frustration before he goes to sleep, just one more lost brown man in England.

In Bombay, it is muggy and sweltering tonight, and Amlan is smoking cigarettes in his car as he drives home on the Bandra-Worli sea link, the sea black sandpaper under the bridge. He misses being thin and being on a motorcycle and being with Nicki. His life, he knows, is now manifestly poorer than it used to be.

Kiran's the same as he always was, as he always will be. He has Swati and he has wrapped his life around her, the way he once wrapped it around Jennifer, like a wire around a magnet. He'll get married to her. His life will always go the way it must. He'll look back on our time together with nostalgia, but it is not his way to create an imaginary world and live half his life in it. He lives in the present and in the future.

Faiza works for one of the FMCG conglomerates, which makes everything from shampoo to chocolate. I last saw her in a bar with a lot of people I've never seen. She looked tired and slack to me. I waved to her but did not stay to chat. I can't imagine what I would have said if I had. We don't really have much in common anymore.

In Delhi, I sit at a barstool, looking at the fingerprints I have left on my drink, the oils my body has exuded on the cold glass. On the screen, Carles Puyol picks up the cup with both hands.

Further east, in Guwahati, Jennifer sits on a bed, bald and thin as they poison her so that she may yet live. Her reality is porous and only her dreams contain any colour. Maybe she dreams of a time when she was beautiful and men fought to love her. Maybe she doesn't dream at all.

In Bangkok, Rathore is lying low. He is probably still lying to people, misguiding, misleading, deceiving. In a strange way, he is closer to his dreams than any of us, living in a never never land of easy drugs and pliable flesh. Maybe he will never return, become another nameless junkie on Khao San Road. But I doubt it.

Malaika's dad pulled a string for her. Now she works for a firm in Singapore. There's an email from her once in a while. For her, that night in that car never ended. The view from the backseat haunts her.

Something wonderful and valuable has happened. I suddenly feel a duty towards meaning. Maybe your life doesn't begin when you're born, or you become an adult, or when people trust you and depend on you, or you have a child. Maybe all of these are good and important things. But maybe, for a human being at least, your life only begins when you realize it means something.

This feeling is the only thing I know worth protecting. Today I feel so alive that I think maybe, if the angel came for me, I would look at my life, look at all the beauty, and go quietly. It's strangely twisted, isn't it, that when you feel life strongest in you, death could be less scary?

At nine-thirty in the morning, I walked into Abhilash's room. 'Abhilash,' I said, 'may I have ten minutes of your time?'

He was in a good mood. 'Of course. Come in.'

I shut the door behind me.

'Is this about how you don't get enough leave again?' Still smiling.

'Sort of,' I said, like a python looking at a fox, something used to being a predator, but way out of scale. 'I want to take a long vacation, boss. I'm quitting.'

Chomp. His eyes widen and his fingers involuntarily splay. He sputters, 'You're going to Dhingra Partners, aren't you? Did they make you an offer?'

'No, I don't have any offers. I'm just quitting.'

'Is it the hours? I know we've been working you very hard.'

'No, no, it's not the hours, Abhilash. I just don't want to do this kind of thing anymore.'

He's silent. 'Do you want to think about this? It's a big step. You could be making a big mistake.'

Right, mate. A massive mistake.

'I've thought about this.'

'So, are you going abroad? Get a degree, work in the States. It's a good life.' He swivels in his chair.

I'm shocked to feel something like sympathy radiating from him. Maybe he's just another guy trying to keep his shit together, to keep his wife in diamonds and his kids in school, trying to keep his head above the waves. However, I do note with satisfaction that he has not sanitized his hands for minutes together.

'Maybe. I haven't figured it out yet.'

I walk out and I feel my big steel balls clanging like temple bells between my legs. I feel eyes on me, partners, associates, inquisitive interns. The cubies here have turned into a carousel – and I'm the centre pole.

Every day associates walk in here, lawyers in their own right, and turn into scribes and instruments. Law firms work on the backs of junior associates. They mill their sweat and hard work and unfulfilled dreams into lucre, and tip them for it. So when an associate walks out the door, something shifts.

Within the week, they'll slot another person, someone as lucky, into my seat. They'll fill in the base of the pyramid with another block and everything will be hunky dory again. But just for today, I think I may have won.

mosquito song

Queens of the Stone Age/Songs for the Deaf/2002

I'm going away for a while.

In the security check line, I blink the sleep from my eyes. All around, I see a phalanx of men in dark suits, with one laptop bag each. Some are Europeans, some Japanese, most are Indian, and they all look exactly the same – the business traveller taking the early morning flight so as to best leverage his time. Each of them removes his coat and puts his mobile phone and wallet in his laptop bag. Then he puts his laptop in a blue tray and his coat and laptop bag in another tray.

And I think, there, but for the grace of god, go I.

I hear the shuddering of small wings above, and look into the upper recesses of the terminal. Perched on the white steel girders in this ultramodern, climate-controlled, painstakingly monitored, secure building is a pigeon. Below it, people raise their arms for the metal detector, shop for watches, eat donuts. It shits serenely on the café tables and on the marble floors.

Looking at it, I sense a great promise. If a pigeon can beat the three layers of glass doors, the air-conditioning, the hundreds of armed men, then there may just be hope for the rest of us, vermin or saint. Surely there must be place in the world for another itinerant, another traveller, another one looking for greatness.

It feels like I have risen from a long sleep and a fever has broken. Suddenly – I want to tell Sasha – I am happy again. I am happy like I used to be when we were younger, walking around barefoot in a loving world. But, for the first time, I feel a sense of agency, like the plot has not been written yet.

I think too of the story I have told. It is bitter, the knowledge that the years to come will be almost certainly more joyous, more ecstatic, more painful, more glorious. It is the prerogative of refugees fleeing the kingdom of youth to imagine themselves coming through slaughter, and then to turn around and see the fabled city glittering on the hill.

I think of Sasha often, and I will think of him yet. But I have now drifted beyond what he could teach me. By the telling of this story, I now feel free of the need to keep him as my oracle. Beyond this point, I must find my own way.

And therefore, here ends my testimony. This is what I saw, and this is my truth. You may think that there are things I have exaggerated, or concealed, that maybe I have said too much. You may imagine that I have perjured myself in the telling. If I have, it is no matter of yours. The truth of it lies only between me and the angel.

acknowledgements

I want to thank my editors – Karthika V.K., who saw something in a manuscript and led me to it; and Ajitha G.S., who guided me with her firm but kind hands, and bore with my interminable phone calls. Thanks also to the team at HarperCollins for being so patient with me.

I am deeply grateful to all those who took the time to read through drafts and give me feedback – Nooreen Sarna, Aditya Sarkar, Yashasvini Kumar, Shloka Vaidialingam, Ravi Singh, Spandan Biswal, Radhika Agrawal, Melissa Zeloof, Deborshi Barat, Prem Mohan, Abhimanyu George Jain.

Thanks to all those who offered encouragement and support – Siddhartha Sen, Vipul Kharbanda, Thomas John, Sulabh Rewari, Tanya Aggarwal, Aditya Sudarshan, Akanksha Singh, Charles and Ariella Zeloof, Arun and Deepa Kumar, Dhruv and Jay Visvanath, Nishita Vasan, Aqseer Sodhi, Dr V.S. Elizabeth, Bikramaditya Bose, Jian Johnson, Neha Mehra, Vikramjeet Singh, Vinay Aravind, Sujay Sanan, Supriya Nair, Aman Sethi, Shahana Chatterjee, Nikhil Singhvi, Pranesh Prakash and many, many others. Thanks especially to my family, who understood.

If I have forgotten anyone, please forgive me.